Saint Jude

by

Dawn Wilson

Tudor Publishers
Greensboro

Saint Jude by Dawn Wilson © 2001

Printed in the United States

First Edition

Cataloging-in-Publication Data

Wilson, Dawn, 1971—
    Saint Jude/by Dawn Wilson
        p.   cm.
    Summary: When committed to an upscale group home outside Asheville, North Carolina, eighteen-year-old Taylor Drysdale pretends that her bipolar disorder is under control and that she will leave soon, but relationships with her fellow residents may hold the key to real recovery.
    ISBN 0-936389-68-0
    [1. Manic-depressive illness—Fiction. 2 .Group homes for the mentally ill. 3. Mental illness-Fiction. 4. Self-mutilation—Fiction. 5. North Carolina—Fiction.] I. Title.

PZ7.W69055 Sai200
[Fic]—dc21
                                                                00-062993

For Mom and Dad

Chapter 1

There's an art to going crazy.

People think that it hits you all at once, but it doesn't. Like regret, it builds up over time, until it drags you out to sea. You make a splash for awhile, but eventually, people forget about you. Then pretty soon, you forget who you are or even if you had ever been.

November was not the time to see Brick House.

The empty, clutching trees and gray sky formed a perfect frame for its aching walls and chipping paint. The front porch was like the crooked back of a junkyard dog. The windows were dingy from lack of activity. The porch swing, broken.

Home for the leftovers. Some way to spend senior year.

Of course, it wasn't even made of bricks. I don't know why they call it Brick House, unless it's loneliness. Bricks are lonely. They sound like they ought to be lonely, anyway.

Mom shifted uneasily. It was her idea. We'd grown hoarse from shouting until it became too painful to even speak. So we stopped. It was just as simple as turning off the lights. Something had snapped, and we both knew better than to try and fix it.

Of course, she had the upper hand because I didn't have my guitar. I was naked without it, and the fingers of my right hand imagined the grooves of the case handle. Mom wouldn't let me bring the guitar until she was sure there was a place where I could keep it locked up. No telling what might happen to it, she said. After all, she had paid two hundred dollars for the thing; it would be senseless for it be stolen or damaged. The porch boards creaked beneath my weight. Mom managed to pack all my things in two suitcases. She had the small one, and I carried the other one, letting the blue vinyl handle etch a design into the crook of my fingers.

She pressed the doorbell, but instead of ringing, it made an awkward clank as if something in its very core was broken beyond repair. A small, bent lady with gray hair tied tightly in a bun answered the door.

"Taylor Drysdale," Mom cleared her throat. "We've brought her stuff, I mean, we're here to settle in."

Her voice had an odd ring to the words, "settle in." The words floated to my stomach and burned.

"Come in," the lady opened the door wide—too wide—like an overly-anxious host who doesn't get too many guests.

Inside a Tar Heel beanbag fought gaudy furniture for attention. There was an impressive wide screen TV with bits of popcorn decorating the dark brown carpet in front of it.

Everything in the room looked as if it were all found at a yard sale; things that someone else didn't want. The couch had an ugly orange, blue and yellow afghan across it that must have been made by a colorblind grandma. The ends of it weren't tied very well, and it was starting to unravel.

"I'll get Mr. Hopkins. He'll be with you in a minute. Please have a seat." With that the lady trotted out of the room, gleefully, like she was heading to take some cookies from the oven.

I didn't want to sit on anything because it looked broken. I was afraid I'd get contaminated and then who'd fix me?

There was a cuckoo clock that fascinated me until I realized that it was a fake. It looked like a real cuckoo, but if you watched it carefully, you'd see that it was made of plastic. The bird in the center was impaled on a stick. It didn't pop out—it just bobbed its head back and forth in a hypnotic dance.

"You need to sit down. You look tired," Mother told me.

I couldn't tell her that if you touched anything in this house you would become broken, too.

"Sit down."

"I can't. I'll get broken, just like the furniture."

"Don't be silly," she remarked. "That's only your Condition talking."

She always referred to it as my "Condition" with a capital "C." Made me sound like I was having my period. "Parent's note: Taylor can't run in P.E. today because she has her Condition."

"Well, where are the people?" I asked. "If this place is so great, then where the hell are the people? Locked up in some room somewhere."

"Taylor, don't swear."

"But where are they?"

"They?" A deep baritone voice called from the stairs. "They are all in a group therapy session. You must be Taylor. We've been expecting you."

To say that he was bald would be an understatement. He jumbled down the steps like a rag doll in a suit and tie. He came to me with an outstretched hand. Instead of shaking his hand, I thumbed through a hymnal on the coffee table. I found that "What a Friend We Have in Jesus" had been ripped out of its place and stuck in the middle like an odd bookmark. I missed my guitar. Mom promised she'd bring it later this week.

"I'm Susan Drysdale," Mom tried her best to make up for my lack of cordiality.

"Arnold Hopkins, director," he said it like he was applying for a job. "Won't you please have a seat?"

"Actually, we really don't have a whole lot of time," she said. She tried to make him think that she was in a hurry, but I knew it was because she was afraid of contamination and getting broken, too. I think he may have picked up on it as well, for he seemed very careful not to touch or brush against anything in the room.

"Certainly, certainly." He had black eyes that shone from

behind oversized glasses. He was stout, but not chubby. He made me nervous, probably because he didn't stop wringing his hands together. His nose was too big, and he looked like a cartoon character drawn badly out of proportion. He reached out his hand again to shake mine. I just stared at him and put my hands in my pockets. He had these huge hands; you could fit a whole football field in there—and rubbing them together. Swish, swish, his palms made squeaky noises because they were obviously sweaty.

"I only brought two suitcases, but I'll bring the rest of her things later on in the week, if that'll be all right."

"The room's all ready, if you'll follow me," his body shuffled toward the staircase. "I think you'll like this room. It has a nice view of the mountains, if you can overlook the junkyard." He gave a laugh that sounded as if it came mostly from his nose.

The room was clean and bare. There was a small desk in the corner of the room and etched onto one of the drawers were the initials "RS and JL." There was a ceiling fan, although I doubted that it worked. There was a white dresser with a reading lamp, and, much to my surprise, a Gideon Bible.

"I'll give you some time to get settled in," he said, opening the closet door in case I hadn't picked up on where the closet was located. "There's a bathroom down the hall on the left. There's a large cabinet in there where you can put your toiletries."

"Thanks." My voice sounded hollow and tinny. I wouldn't have recognized it as mine.

He gave a crooked half-smile and left the room, arms dangling. He pulled the door, leaving it slightly cracked.

"We can go now," I said. "We can get the deposit back and everything can go back the way it was."

"That's just it, Taylor. Have you forgotten the way things were?"

"But I can control it this time. Just give me a chance."

"How many chances does it take? What is it going to take to prove to you that you can't handle this? When you end up in an institution? That's where you're heading."

I was determined for her not to see me cry. I bit my lip. Institution. She had no idea. Two weeks in the hospital. Big deal. I know people who've had worse.

She gave me an awkward kiss on the cheek and then left, closing the door behind her. I could hear the thud of her feet going down the steps. I stared out the window—which did have a lovely view of both the mountains and a junkyard—until I saw her thin, willowy form exit. I placed my suitcase on the bed and unpacked.

"You getting settled, dear?" a voice called from the door. "If you don't mind, we prefer for the first couple of weeks, you keep the door open. Except when you're getting dressed." It was the lady who welcomed us into the house.

"I'd like to have my privacy."

"Of course, and we want you to have your privacy, but all in good time, dear. All in good time."

I threw some panties into one of the dresser drawers. The drawer looked worn and musty. I briefly debated whether or not I wanted my underwear to be touching it.

"My name is Maria Lupe Rodriquez Merano," she said. "But around here folks call me Big Mama."

"Hi." There was no way in hell I was going to call her "mama" anything.

"Have you unpacked your things?"

"Just started."

"I wish I had gotten up here before you opened your suitcase. It would have saved you some trouble." She opened the drawers and started going through all my clothes, even my underwear.

"What are you doing?"

"Looking for sharps, dear. Have to check everyone. It's the rules, you know."

"Sharps?"

"Scissors, nail files . . ." she pried into my toiletry case and triumphantly held up my razor, " . . . razors," there was a hint of pride in her voice.

"So what? I shave my legs."

"Not without supervision. You might want to consider getting an electric razor."

"I am not going to have someone sit and watch me shave my legs."

"It's just a precaution, dear. Just for the first couple of weeks until we get a better profile of you."

"I'll just have hairy legs then."

"Suit yourself."

She moved on to my hair dryer and curling iron.

"These have got to go, too," she said, wrapping the cords around her wrist.

"Why? They aren't sharp."

"Choking," she stretched out the cord to illustrate her point. "We had a girl nearly commit suicide by rigging up a noose with a hair dryer cord."

"I'm not going to do anything like that."

"Of course you're not, dear. It's just that we want to be sure that you're safe."

"Safe from what?"

"Yourself."

She picked through my stuff like a shopper at a K-mart blue light special. She checked the pockets of all my blue jeans and even felt down in my socks in case I was stashing a grenade in there.

"Are those the only pair of earrings you brought with you?"

"Yes."

She tilted her head and took a closer look at them. Then she stretched out her hand.

"You'll have to give those to me."

"You're afraid I'm going to choke on it or something?"

"It's the backs," she took the earring and ran the back of it up and down her arm, making a pink streak. "You'd be surprised how people can cut themselves on these."

"Okay, okay, just do what you have to and get out." I sat on the corner of the bed.

Big Mama sat beside me.

"I know you didn't want to come here. But forget about what you've heard about this place or what you think that it might be. It sounds hokey, I know, but we really are a family here. And here you'll have little friends who are struggling with the same things you are."

I wanted to tell her to kiss off, but I was afraid if I told her, she'd only stick around to argue, and I wanted to get rid of her as soon as possible.

She shuffled through the rest of my things as dutifully as a prison matron. She took my compact because she said the mirror inside could be broken to form sharp edges. I noticed the clothes hangers in the closet were permanently attached to the rod, like the kind you see in hotels.

I didn't hear her leave. I crashed my fists into a pillow on the bed, looking out the window over the junkyard.

Even with the spectacular view of the mountains, it was the junkyard that fascinated me. On the heap was an old blue Pinto, cinder blocks replacing its wheels. I felt sorry for it because I realized that it and I were the same. The forgotten. Tossed into a scrap yard for improvements. Of course everyone told me this was for my own good, yet I felt that someone fed that same line to the Pinto and look at it— a pathetic wash of nuts and bolts that couldn't go anywhere unless God Himself had a hand in it.

I can't even say I was really upset when the diagnosis came down. Bipolar disorder. Of course, I had heard of manic-depression, even studied it in my psychology class, but the faces in the videotape seemed so unreal, surely they couldn't apply to me.

Then came the spending sprees and the cold nights of crying . . .

"What do you want on your pizza?" It was a boyish figure sporting John Lennon glasses and short red hair that was styled in a man's haircut.

"What?"

"It's Friday," she said impatiently. "Pizza night. What do you want on it?"

"I don't know. What everybody else has will be okay."

"Better not say that. Isaac likes anchovies on his."

"Anything except black olives."

"Gotcha. By the way, I'm Reno. You're the new admit, aren't you?"

"Word travels fast."

"Boy, are you lucky. Just missed the most murderous hour of group therapy I've ever been through." She grabbed her throat and made gagging noises. "What's your name? Never mind, I'll find out soon enough. Oh, by the way, Big Mama wants you to help her set the table."

"Great."

"Hey, be nice to Big Mama. She's the one you need to drive you around places. Think she's a sweet little old lady? Piss her off and see how far you get. It's worse than being grounded."

Reno tucked her head out of the door and I heard her brisk footsteps dart down the hallway. I pulled out of bed. My head had a particular ache to it, the kind you have when you're getting the flu.

I was stumbling down the steps when I first heard the humming in the walls, like there was machinery inside them and the house was starting to come alive.

I followed the voices to the kitchen. There was a small dining room with a long table with mix-and-match chairs. A picnic bench filled in for some of the missing chairs. A pink tablecloth seemed to be linen, but on closer examination it proved to be cheap plastic, like the kind used to paper church fellowship hall tables during covered-dish dinners.

Voices were everywhere. Scurrying, building around me in vague crescendos of blue and green. Somewhere among them was the familiar street-tough whine of Reno, muttering something about mushrooms and black olives. It's all misty-like, kind of wispy and warm like the bathroom when you step out of the shower. Then the break:

"Hey, it's what's-her-face," said Reno, ending her conversation with Big Mama and heading toward me. "May I have your attention, please?" she said in a voice sound lower than natural. "May I give you the obvious pleasure of introducing to you the charter member of the Reno Shepherd Fan Club? What's-her-face from Lickskillet, Oklahoma."

This was greeted by a round of boos and hisses.

"Hey, now, I know you all wanted to be charter members, but we had to leave that to Linda here."

"Linda?" called a skinny, sandy-haired guy in the corner. "Is that her name?"

"Ah, ah, ah," she covered my mouth with her hand. "Just how much is it worth to you? Who wants to place bets on what her name is?"

"You're crazy," he said.

"No shit, Sherlock. Why do you think we're all in Brick House? Now who wants to place a bet? I'll place thirty minutes on Linda."

"It's fixed," a squatty guy chimed in. "You've looked at her records."

"You know Daddy Warbucks would prefer to be be gift-wrapped naked and sent to hell than to let any of us get our paws on those records."

"Daddy Warbucks?" I asked.

"Mr. Hopkins. We call him that because he's bald, in case you didn't notice. We also call him Big Daddy."

"I mean, I have seen bald men in my time but that guy

is *bald*." The squatty guy got a Coke from the fridge. "I mean balder than bald. It's like his head has some kind of nuclear fallout that kills the hairs before they even start to grow."

"The woman's wig we gave him for Christmas. That was cruel." It is the sandy-haired guy again. He's almost blonde and his long bangs reveal where the sun had streaked its fingers across his hair.

"And you are?" I asked because he was kind of cute.

"Allow me," Reno stepped in with a flourish of her arm. "This is my esteemed colleague, Brad Pitt. Mr. Pitt, I loved your latest movie, but found, sadly, that you did not show your butt nearly enough. For your next film perhaps, oh, just do your next film in the buff. And this," she jumped over to the squatty guy, who had already downed his Coke and was starting on another, "is Elvis. Yes, he's alive and has been at Brick House to keep out of the limelight.

"And Princess . . ." Reno's voice trailed off. "Princess is late as usual because Princess has extra leave privileges and is probably wreaking havoc on a shopping mall somewhere."

"Who's Princess?" I asked.

"A rich bitch," Brad Pitt replied flatly.

"Now, Blaine," Big Mama admonished as she trotted into the kitchen. I could tell everyone was wondering how long she had been listening, "Deana is no different from anyone else. And she hates it when you call her Princess."

"But that's what she looks like," Reno squealed. "How can you look at that two-inch waist and those breasts that should be national landmarks and not think of some skinny, spoiled rich, fairy-tale-till-you-throw-up princess?"

"Falsies, don't you bet," Brad Pitt chimed.

"Now, now, children." Big Mama was not pleased.

I went through the cabinets, looking for silverware to set the table, but all I found were those plastic spoon/fork combinations you get at Kentucky Fried Chicken.

"Where's the silverware?"

"In here," Brad Pitt rattled a drawer at the far end of the kitchen. "Locked. You see, they're afraid we might get a hold of one of the knives or forks and get a little crazy."

"But what I don't understand is why they keep the spoons locked up as well," Reno complained. "I mean, who ever hurt someone with a spoon?"

She took one of the plastic spoon/forks and grabbed Brad Pitt from behind, as if she were holding a knife at his throat. Brad went along with it and started crying hysterically.

"Don't anyone move. I've got one of the spoon/fork things," Reno tried to muster up a gangster voice. "One false move and pretty boy here gets it."

There's a round of laughter, but it's nervous laughter, as if laughing really isn't allowed in the house. So everyone just let out a half-hearted chuckle, then looked anxiously around to see if someone heard it.

"Let's go, Taylor." Big Mama gathered some dishes and headed for the dining room table.

"Taylor! Aha! So her name isn't Linda after all. You lost the bet," Elvis suddenly became animated.

"We never officially bet on it. I made the offer, but no one was interested. So there was never really any bet. Deal with it," she responded.

I tried to avoid Big Mama's eyes. They were cold and gray. There was something hardheaded about her, like a woman who had spent one too many years living and was now paying the price.

The dishes weren't real dishes. They were these plastic plates that were a sickly shade of orange. Once again, unbreakable.

Big Daddy or Daddy Warbucks or whatever they called him returned with the pizza and spread it on the table like a Thanksgiving turkey. It had black olives. We dutifully took our places at the table, with Big Daddy at the head and Big Mama across from him.

"Would anyone like to volunteer to say grace?" he asked.

Sensing my puzzled look, he quickly added, "Not that we push a certain kind of religion over another, but the local Catholic church makes many valuable contributions to the home, and, well, we figure the least we can do is say grace."

Brad Pitt volunteered.

"Yea, God. Boo, Devil. Amen."

And everyone was okay with that.

The pizza tasted cold and stale even though I knew it was fresh. I spent most of my time picking off the black olives and piling them in an odd pyramid on the side of my plate. There was some talk of school, of homework, of how it sucked to be dateless on a Friday night. But Friday night was movie night, and Big Daddy insisted that they would like the feature that he had picked for this evening. There was a collective groan.

"Just once, would it kill you to pick up an R-rated movie?" Reno asked.

"Don't you think your minds have been polluted enough?" Big Daddy seemed unfazed. "You see, Taylor, here we see ourselves as a community, a family, if you will. Because we are all dealing with a wide range of psychological problems, it is important that we take daily temperature readings to see how we're getting along as a community, so we can stop any problems before they start. Our community meetings present a good time to vent any frustrations you have with the way the home is run. It's an open forum."

Later, dishes were cleared and we set chairs in a circle in the living room. A tall, thin blonde entered the room. I could only assume that she was Princess; she had breasts that were large and menacing.

Big Daddy took the helm and waited for the others to be seated. He scratched his head and set a legal pad on his lap.

"Well," he cleared his throat, "as we all know by now, this is Taylor Drysdale. She will be staying in what was Joan's old room. Taylor just joined us today."

There was a unified grumble through the group.

"How are we all doing? Isaac, how was that chemistry test?"
Elvis answered. "I was a bit distracted."

"Did your affective disorder cause problems?"

"No, the blonde in the third row," he winked and elbowed
Brad Pitt.

"And speaking of women, how are you dealing with your
break up, Blaine?"

"It's her loss," he said. "She didn't want to go out with
me when she found out that I was crazy. At first that bothered
me, but now, I don't care who knows. If they can't deal with
it, screw 'em. I don't need them messing with me."

There was a short silence. The tall blonde that had joined
the group lit a cigarette and took a long drag.

"Deana, there is no smoking in the house."

"Cut me some slack, okay? Let me have my thrill." Her
clothes looked as if they had been taken from the mannequin
at The Limited. Everything matched, from the pale pink of her
lipstick to the pink of her nail polish and the pink of the broach
she wore on her collar.

"Deana, please introduce yourself."

"My name's Deana Hays and I've been at Brick House off
and on for five months, and that's five months too long. I can't
tell you what's wrong with me, because nobody really knows."
She paused and took another drag on the cigarette, in open de-
fiance of Big Daddy. "And if you ever, *ever* call me Princess,
I will scratch your eyes out."

As if they had been given a cue, the group began to chant
"Princess . . . Princess. . . Princess."

"Oh, knock it off!" She flipped some ashes in their direction. "It's bad enough I have to live with you nut cases."

"Reno?" Big Daddy looked at her hopefully, thinking that
she would provide a change to the tension that Princess un-
leashed upon the group.

"Smooth sailing. I'm the Prozac poster child," she smiled—
a wiry, toothy grin.

And so the wheel rolled to me. I looked at the gallery of faces. What did they want from me? It was all a game. Brick House, the group therapy sessions, everything was a game.

"I'm manic depressive," I said curtly, as if that should be all they needed to know.

"Is there any community business that needs to be brought up?"

"I have a question," Isaac said. "Why is it we have to get up at eight on Saturdays? I mean, couldn't we sleep late one day a week?"

"That is an excellent question, Mr. Peterson," Big Daddy crossed and uncrossed his legs. "A great deal of time and planning went into the schedule. We thought it would be best to get up early so you could do your chores and get them over so you could enjoy Saturday night with your little friends. After you finish your chores, it's a free day. You can go back to bed if you like."

"Besides, sleep too late and you'll miss Bugs Bunny," Reno said.

"But, if you like, Big Mama and I will review the schedule and see if we couldn't allow some extra hours here and there for sleep."

"That would be great."

"Is there any further business? Deana, for the last time put out that cigarette before I assign you some hours. Nothing else? Okay, movie starts at eight."

"What did you get?"

"*Mary Poppins.*"

"Warbucks." Blaine waved his hand in the air. "How many times do we have to tell you that past a certain age Disney is just not cool."

"Would you like to have a film committee?"

"Definitely."

"Then head one up. Next week someone else can get the movie. I'm tired of hearing you whine."

I placed my chair back to its original position at the dining room table.

"Taylor, may I see you for a moment in my office, just to go through some orientation stuff?" Big Daddy said it as if I had no other option.

His office was located in the back side of the house near his bedroom. It was bleak and bare, save for a full color map of the Great Smoky Mountains National Park. He motioned me toward a seat that gave a soft poot as I sat down.

"I know we're hitting you with a lot of information all at once," he began, "but you're a smart kid and I know you can handle it. Let's see, Drysdale, Taylor Jay Drysdale . . ." he pulled a file from his desk. "You are eighteen years old. You had a sister who died in a car accident when you were nine. Your parents divorced when you were twelve. You started seeing a doctor three years ago for severe chest pain. After all tests came back normal, he ruled it psychosomatic and sent you to a psychiatrist. At times you can stay up for three days at a time, and on other occasions all you want to do is sleep.

"Psychological testing revealed atypical bipolar disorder, or manic depression. Started taking lithium two months ago but still having problems." He peered at me over his glasses as if waiting for approval to go on. I nodded slightly.

"Taylor, do you know how Brick House operates?"

I shook my head. I decided the less I said, the better.

"First of all, it's not Brick House. I know that's what everybody calls it. I think it's taken from an incident three years ago when the football team got suspended for throwing bricks through the windows. It's real name is Saint Jude's Academy. We're an experiment, really. We've only been around for four years. We knew some young people with mental illnesses were slipping through the cracks in the mental health system. Many are not bad enough to go to a hospital or group home. Many are able to function in society. But they are volatile and their balance rests on a small hinge. We have immediate access to a psychiatrist if you have a relapse. We offer group therapy and individual therapy every day, just like a hospital would."

"When can I go home?" I uttered the words before I could hold them back.

"You are free to come and go as you please. However, we must maintain a strict account of where you'll be, when, and for how long. We reserve the right to keep you from going places that we deem psychologically unhealthy. All transportation must be arranged with Big Mama a week in advance.

"Since you are new, you do not have leave privileges yet. As we develop a deeper sense of trust toward you and evaluate your psychological condition, we will start with three hours a week and then take it from there.

"You will be assigned hours, or chores, which you must do every week. If you violate the rules of Saint Jude's, you will be assigned extra hours of work or your leave privileges will be revoked. Here's a booklet with the list of rules. Take some time to read them over."

"I'll need to go home and get my guitar."

"Please do not think of this as a group home," he prattled on without skipping a beat. "We like to think of Saint Jude's as a family. Now are there any questions?"

His words seemed to hover in the air for a long time after he had spoken them.

"When can I go home?" It was worth repeating.

"Once we determine your mood has been stabilized for a sufficient period of time. But Taylor, for right now, this is your home."

Home? I was in a foreign country. I was hovering somewhere in between the real world and this pseudo-hospital ward. Big Daddy removed his glasses and wiped off a spot with the edge of his tie. I knew those eyes would be watching every move I made.

Chapter 2

Welcome to Saint Jude's. This booklet is an outline of rules and regulations for members—you are not considered patients. We like to think of Saint Jude's as a family.

"She's reading it. I can't get over it, she's actually reading it. Taylor, don't you have something better to do? I mean, even *Mary Poppins* is better than that," Reno was tossing popcorn into her mouth in short, sharp spurts, like a machine gun as her eyes gazed halfheartedly at the scene taking place on the wide-screen TV.

"Shut up, Reno, here's where they go to cartoonland."

"Oh, back off my butt, Isaac, I know you're not watching it, either."

"When I get my film committee together, Disney will be the first to go," Blaine said, after quickly taking a glance to be sure Big Mama and Big Daddy were out of the room.

"Thank God for the film committee. I wonder why he didn't let us have one sooner?" Reno said.

"It's a power play," Isaac dove into the popcorn. "He controls what we see, he controls what we think. It's all because the Catholic church gives us so much money. I'll bet he has a blacklist of movies we aren't allowed to see. Hey, Blaine, think we can get any of those naked stewardess movies?"

"Nah, man, you got to start small. Go with the little victories, and then, when you're least expecting it, WHAM—in slips something a little questionable. But we got to start small. Who wants to be on my committee?"

"I will!" Isaac raised his hand. "Walt Disney, your days are numbered."

"Count me in," Reno said. "But I want equal air time. If we have naked stewardesses, I want naked pilots, too."

"Should I go ask Princess?" Isaac asked.

"You just want a chance to be alone with her so you can try to get at her chest."

"Me?" He raised his eyebrows. "Not me, man. You could smother in boobs that big."

"What about you, Taylor? Want to be on the committee?"

"I dunno. I don't guess so."

"Come on, think of it. Your pick of any flick you want."

"I don't have time."

"Sweetheart," Blaine chuckled as he slapped my knee, "at Brick House, all you've got is time. We are limited to only one extracurricular activity per school semester. That way Big Mama doesn't go crazy toting us all over the county."

"It also gives us time to regain our mental health," Reno said in a deep voice, as if she were imitating Big Daddy. "And I think the first order of business for the film committee is to have a *Captain Kangaroo* film festival."

"Hey!" Blaine sprang to her side. "What would you think of an Oscar party?"

"An Oscar party?"

"Yeah, the night of the Oscars, we get all duded up, rent tuxedos or something, and have a party while we stay up and watch the Oscars."

"Big Daddy'll never go for it. The Oscars are always on a school night."

My new world became billowy and shaky, like it was all underwater. Or like the fireworks at the state fair, little sparks going off, never really making any sense in their own right, but somehow fusing together into a network, creating its own world, one of spitfire and sass. One that burns too brightly and then fades as it falls to earth.

On my way upstairs Reno warned me I'd miss the end of
the movie. I mumbled something to the fact that I had seen
it before when I was six. I passed by the first bedroom on my
right. Princess was sitting on the bed, painting her toenails the
exact shade of pink to match her blouse. Her eyes were puffy
and swollen as if she had been crying.

"What are you staring at?" she bit back at me.

"Nothing."

"Get out of my face. I don't need a whacko like you on
this hall."

She wouldn't have said that if Big Daddy or Big Mama
were around. I went to my bedroom window. The night had
covered the mountains. However, in the light of the moon, I
could just make out the old Pinto sitting on the cinder blocks,
crying for a master.

Chapter 3

Lights will be out promptly at 10 p.m. At Saint Jude, it is important that we adhere to all guidelines so we may function as a community. Young men will sleep on the first floor, the young ladies upstairs. We will treat you as adults until you give us reason to do otherwise . . .

Noise filtered around my head; a soupy fog from a Stephen King movie. I pulled myself out of bed. Laughter. Light filters through the open door. I tried to go back to sleep, but it's almost impossible to sleep with somebody laughing, because deep inside you wonder if they're laughing at you. I pulled my blue terrycloth robe over my shoulders. I stumbled toward the light.

"Hey, wake up, sleepy head. We were wondering when you were going to join us."

I squinted, the light was too bright. Voices seemed to come from all around me.

"Pull up a seat and join the round table."

I felt a hand reach up and grab the belt around my robe.

"What's going on?" The three of them gathered in a semi-circle in the middle of the hallway.

"It's a Campfire Girls meeting," Reno said. "In case you haven't guessed, guys aren't allowed up here. So every Friday night we break the rules and have some old-fashioned bonding. It's like *Oprah* without the audience."

"And on this occasion," Blaine said with a flair, "I managed to clean out the candy machine for all it was worth. If you hit it just right, the candy'll fall down and the machine gives you the money back."

He tossed me a Snickers bar. I took it gingerly and placed it in the pocket of my robe.

"So where were we? Reno, I think it's your turn to pick a subject."

"Yes, yes, yes. What is the most unusual place you've ever made out? Blaine?"

"It was actually in the girl's locker room during a basketball game."

"I'll bet there were lots of personal fouls," Reno grinned and elbowed me.

"It was in the shower stall. Halfway through she backed me up against the wall and I accidentally turned on the cold water."

"And he's been taking cold showers ever since," Isaac said. "Isaac?"

He cleared his throat and spread his arms wide as if we were in store for a big production. "In Manhattan, in the Macy's Thanksgiving Day Parade!"

Cries of protest and disbelief erupted—they had to shush themselves lest Mama or Warbucks hear.

"You weren't in Macy's Thanksgiving Day parade," Blaine threw an M&M at him. "Much less fooling around in one."

"It's true, I swear."

"So . . ." Reno bit off a piece of licorice and twirled it between her thumb and forefinger. "Where were you?"

"In New York."

"Oh, like, duh. I meant where were you in the parade? You weren't making out while trying to hold up that big Woody Woodpecker balloon, were you?"

"I was on a float."

"There were tons of floats. Which one were you on?"

"I was on the one with the cast from *Little Shop of Horrors*. I was in the plant suit. With a girl. All I had to do was just wave my arms so it looked like the plant was moving."

"There was room for two people in there?"

"We made room."

"I still don't believe it," Reno ate the rest of her licorice. "Sorry. It just doesn't add up."

"But it's true. I couldn't make that up. I'm not that creative. Or that smart, for that matter."

"Reno, he does have a point," Blaine said.

"I say we put it to a vote," she pounded her fist as if it were a make-believe gavel. "Hear ye, hear ye, in this matter before the court docket number 35241, motions for summary judgment denied, and the matter will be taken up before the jury. Those members of the 'Castaways' will vote on whether or not the aforesaid member did or did not participate in avid necking in the Macy's Thanksgiving Day parade."

"I say he did it," Blaine patted Isaac on the shoulder admiringly, "because he has guts. Guts of steel. Yes, he did it."

"He's full of shit," Reno said, drawing out "shit" until it was four or five syllables long.

They looked at me expectantly, as if I had a role to play in this.

"Taylor, you're the deciding vote. What do you say?" Reno asked.

"I—I don't know enough about the case to decide."

"Come on," Blaine interjected.

"Can I abstain?"

"Abstention," Reno pointed her finger and looked down at me. "Abstention is a very dirty word. You must decide. If you go through life abstaining on everything, you find out too soon that your life hasn't been worth a damn. Take a stand. Vote."

"I'd have to know more facts."

"Facts?" Reno raised one eyebrow. "Honey, you want facts, I'll give them to you. Blaine: schizophrenic. Been in and out of hospitals since he was what, eleven?"

"Thirteen," Blaine corrected.

"Isaac has schizo-affective disorder. That's a special name

they give when they don't know what's wrong with you. Keeps
them from looking like idiots. As for me, I'm *just* depressed."
She placed an odd emphasis on the word "just" "You have the
facts. Now vote."

"Yeah, but how did you approach this girl?" I asked. "Just
'hey babe, how about you and me doing it in a plant suit for
the Macy's parade? I'll show you what I'm thankful for?'"

"She was going out of town," Isaac said, "and I had promised a friend I'd stand in on the plant for him. It was the
only time we had together. It was now or never."

"Did you do it all through the parade, or only when the
float was stopped?"

"What are you, going to be a reporter or something"

"Time's up, Lois Lane," Blaine called the question. "Vote."
There was only one way out.

"I vote one-half. I believe he did it in the parade, but it
was on the float with the cast from *Cats*. Not in a plant suit."

"Gentlemen, I think we have a new Castaway," Reno an-
nounced. The guys cried "yes, yes" and started to clap.

"Is that something good?" I'm afraid to ask what it is. Only
more lunacy. Sexuality in showers and parades, Walt Disney
on the Friday night movie. Brick House must be a jigsaw puzzle of returns, of irregulars, of misplaced car keys under sofa
cushions. It would be best to join in the clatter of what went
on around me, like an out-of-tune circus act involving clowns
and banana cream pies. To be out would mean to be out of
the loop, out of touch, exorcised from the world that was supposed to be mine. To be out would mean to be cut up and
cut off. Even if it was cut off from this rag-tag group—they
were *my* rag-tags. To lose their favor would be lose the favor
of those who I would have to live with. They had the power
to make Brick House heaven or hell, and they knew it, oh they
knew it, with their paper smiles and untrained antics. Their feigns
of insanity growing to swelling waves that court you to either
flow with them or drown. Drown in what? Self-pity? Mostly.

Self-loathing? Some. Self-mutilation? We'll see.

"Taylor, what you don't realize is that by simply being at Brick House you are already a Castaway. All you need is to get your official club name and you can join the crew here on the *S.S. Minnow*," Reno said. "All together now."

In a broken-hearted chorus, they sang the theme for *Gilligan's Island*.

An opening door broke the melody and an infuriated, albeit muddled, Princess loomed over the circle.

"For the love of God, will you shut up!" Her eyes darted around like maniacal little rodents. "And what are boys doing here? You know they're not allowed up here."

"If I had my way, you wouldn't be allowed up here," Reno was building up steam. This is why I didn't risk rejection. This is why I went along without question. Princess was cut off, and now the wave was going to pull her underwater.

"I'm writing you up for this," Princess said.

"She won't listen to you. She's sick of you writing us up for everything we do. You'd write us up for breathing."

"Maybe if you weren't so obnoxious . . ."

"Maybe if you weren't such a bitch."

Isaac cupped his hand to his mouth and started to murmur "cat fight, cat fight." I'm the most nervous because I'm sitting between them. No way I was going to get in a fight between two crazy people.

"Why do you have to treat me this way?" Her hair was a tousled mess, slithering hither and fro like a blonde Medusa. "You're all a bunch of losers. You don't matter to anyone and that's why you're left here."

"Us? What about you? You're here, too." Reno had taken up arms as the spokesperson for the group.

"Daddy comes for me. I only stay here a couple of months a year when I need rest for my nervous condition. Mom takes me shopping. Sister lets me stay with her in her condo at the beach. I drive a Mercedes. You probably haven't even touched one, I'll bet." She sat back, smiling smugly.

"No, Princess, we aren't spoiled rich. We're just middle class white trash. Hey, Isaac, did you know we were white trash?"

"No, Reno, I didn't know we were trash."

"You, Blaine?"

"I didn't know—"

"Just shut up!" Princess pounded her fists on her temples and for a while I thought she was pulling her hair out. "Will you just stop your stupid songs and let me go to bed? And I'm not Princess, my name's Deana. If you can't call me that then—then—"

"Then you'll what?"

"Don't." A long, manicured finger held Reno as its target. "I'll make you sorry you even met me."

"I already am."

With a flourish of her silk robe she scurried, flustered, into her room and slammed the door. No one said anything for a while for fear that the door had awakened Big Mama and Big Daddy. Reno didn't dare breathe. I know because I'm watching for the faint rising and falling of her chest, as if knowing that Reno was still working would mean all was right with the world. But she didn't. She held her breath, nostrils flared slightly. She broke into a glaring grin.

"I say we tie her down, force her into some horrible seventies clothes, drive her out to Tennessee, and leave her there."

Reno's suggestion met with the thumbs-up approval from the guys.

"But now, to answer Taylor's question before we were so rudely interrupted," Reno continued. "We are the Castaways. Just like the ones on TV. This is how it started: Big Daddy had rented one of those Disney classics and we were bored to the point of tears. We discussed philosophical issues, such as the meaning of life, how to deal with our mental illness, and the Great Question about *Gilligan's Island.*"

"Which is?"

"If the professor is so smart and he can make a bicycle out of coconuts, why doesn't he just fix the boat and go home?"

"It's a question that always kept me awake at night," Isaac muttered.

"So we debate, and we come up with a solution," Reno held her palms in the air as if to frame a thought balloon. "The professor is gay, only he doesn't know it yet. That explains his inability to choose between Ginger and Mary Ann. The professor knows that going back to the real world would mean confronting his sexuality, and he's not ready to do that yet. So he allows Gilligan to jinx all his plans."

"Then we really started thinking about it, and you know what? All those Castaways people were really nuts," Isaac said. "We assigned them all mental disorders. Like Skipper, he's passive aggressive; the frustrations he has with Gilligan are really frustrations that he has with himself. Ginger is narcissistic. The Howells are obsessive-compulsive. I mean, look at all that stuff they brought for a three-hour tour."

"Gilligan is a klutz because he's had too many electroshock treatments and his brain is fried," Reno added. "Kind of like me. And Mary Ann, you just think she's all nice and innocent. But really she has her kinky love with whips and chains. We are the Castaways. We're stranded at Saint Jude's just like they were stranded on an island. I'm Gilligan because I get ECT treatments."

Blaine reached over and put a finger to her temple. "Zap!" he cried, and Reno started going into fake convulsions.

"It's not so bad," she said. "But you end up with a hell of a headache later."

"I'm Skipper," Blaine said. "Isaac is Mr. Howell. Now we have to come up with a Castaway for you."

"Who's Princess?" I asked.

A scowl crossed Reno's face. "Princess is nobody. She's too good to cater to our juvenile games. She's too busy polishing the fenders on her BMW or Mercedes or whatever it is.

I'll tell it to you now, kid. Princess is bad news. She only cares about herself. Worst of all, she's not even sick."

"What do you mean?"

"I mean she's faking it to get attention from mommy and daddy. There's nothing wrong with her. She's no more depressed than the average Joe you'd meet on the street."

"Then how did she get in here?"

"Daddy is a big shot on the board of Brick House. He goes to the church that started it—the very wealthy church that started it—and he has made several sizable donations to Brick House. If it weren't for him, the house wouldn't be able to operate."

"So when Princess has trouble, his big bucks are enough to just let her in?"

"How are you going to say no to the man who gave over fifty thousand dollars to Brick House last year?" Reno said.

"Fifty thousand?"

"Or something like that."

"Is that why she gets to leave whenever she wants?"

"And she usually chooses chore time to leave. She can do anything she wants. If daddy doesn't let her go out to a party, she develops this 'nervous condition.' It gets so bad, she has to go to Brick House. In a few days, daddy changes his mind and she goes home. I've seen the pattern over and over so many times it makes me want to puke."

"And they allow that?"

"She even got the nicest room!" Reno nearly shouted it. "That used to be my room until Princess developed her nervous condition. They moved me out so she could have the best room. Bastards. You know, I think she's had a nose job since she started coming here. And the tits, you know the tits have got to be fake. If there's a problem, just throw money at it. Must be nice."

"It wouldn't be so bad if she weren't such a jerk," Blaine said. "She's always reminding you of how bad she's got it and how much better she is than you. She doesn't know the first thing about mental illness. I lost three part-time jobs because of my schizophrenia before they found the right medicine combination. I failed the twelfth grade and I'm having to repeat it this year. I was too sick to make it up in summer school. Not counting all the doctor's bills that it took to get this thing diagnosed. Mom put me in Brick House because I'm still somewhat unstable. Like one of those crystals that if you hit it at just the right place, it'll shatter into a thousand pieces."

"I'm just here because I'm a pain," Reno said. "I have some kind of depression, working on a personality disorder, and in-between times I made life miserable for my parents. They were glad to get rid of me. Send me off somewhere before I get into trouble or become a juvenile delinquent. I have my problems but I'm not as bad as these two guys are. They're nuts."

Blaine and Isaac just laughed, as if, coming from Reno, it was a compliment.

"So what about you?" Blaine turned a skeptical eye in my direction. "Why did you really come here?"

"Oh, I won't be here long. Mom just wanted me to have a place to stay until I got my mood stabilized. That's all. I'll be gone within two weeks."

"That's what I said," Reno cleared her throat.

"But I won't stay—"

"Once you're here, Big Daddy decides how long you'll stay. If you're trying to get out of here quickly, let me save you some time and tell you that it won't happen. No one has stayed in here shorter than seven months except for Princess and we all know where she pulls her strings."

"But back to the Castaways. Who should Taylor be?" Isaac asked.

"Well, she's in Joan's old room, so why don't we name her Mary Ann after Joan. She has that wholesome American-as-apple-pie-but-don't-screw-with-me look," Blaine said.

"Who's Joan?"

An odd silence settled over the group. They looked at the

floor, the walls, the roof, anything but me. Isaac started to draw patterns on the floor with his finger. Blaine cleared his throat.

"Joan was before you got here. She was manic-depressive, too. But she—"

"Graduated." Reno looked up as if she had been meditating. "She graduated from Brick House and has gone on to far better things."

Again the silence settled like a deep fog. I found myself becoming lost in it. My ears strained to hear the hum of a furnace or the creaks of the old building.

"You would have really liked Joan. She was—"

"Let's not talk about Joan," Reno interrupted Blaine. There was a dark seriousness to her voice that I had never heard before. "It's late. I have to get up early and fix breakfast. Big Mama has the day off."

"Will you make those pancakes in the silhouettes of cartoon characters?"

"I certainly will." The old lilt was back to her voice.

The group shuffled, flickered and dispersed. I felt like I'd taken a long trip somewhere but my room is less than five feet away. I stared at the hallway, now blank and bleak without the Castaways to breathe life into it. I wandered back to my room, still listening for any creaks or sputters of the floors and walls, but it was a quiet house.

Chapter 4

*You are expected to be up and dressed for breakfast by 7:30
a.m. on weekdays and 8:30 a.m. on weekends . . .*

Sunlight seeped its way through the cracks in my mind. I
draped the pillow over my eyes. The light glowed on the inside of my closed eyelids, making odd shapes and colors. Rem-
nants of dreams stagnated within my brain and begged to be
left center stage. Chatter from last night still rattled in my ears.

"Hey!" Princess' voice barks into my ears.

I turned. Her toy store frame came into focus, fuzzy around
the edges, like a bad photograph.

"You overslept."

What was last night? An initiation? A dress rehearsal? It
was something more. They were checking me out to see if I
was like them or like Princess. I fumbled down the stairs.

"Well, looky who's here. I'll get your pancakes." Reno's
voice is far too chipper for mornings. "I'll make you a pancake in the shape of your favorite cartoon character. What'll
it be? Scooby Doo? Fred Flintstone?"

My eyes bothered me. I rubbed them roughly, hoping they'd
water over and clean themselves since I didn't have time to
wash my face this morning.

"Okay, Taylor, it's late morning, time to come alive."

"I didn't sleep well last night."

"Yeah," she giggled. "I'll bet you didn't. So come on, who'll
it be? Superman?"

"Bugs Bunny," I said it just to pacify her.

"One of my personal favorites," Reno trotted back into the kitchen where I found the bowl of batter still on the counter.

"They've promoted me." She tied a red apron around her twig of a waistline. "When I first came here, they didn't let me cook, wouldn't let me near a hot object — it was too dangerous. But I graduated. Now they let me cook on Saturday. It gives Big Mama some time off."

With a flick of her wrist, she placed the batter in droplets onto the skillet in the form of rabbit ears. "Cooking is my passion. Just ask Blaine about my homemade black bean dip. You could kill a man for it."

I got uneasy when she said the word "kill." It wrapped its way around her lips like something from Victoria's Secret. Too comfortable too soon.

Big Daddy dressed casually, with a button-down Oxford and brown Dockers. I gritted my teeth and my jaw froze.

"Taylor," he said, laying a hand on my shoulder, "group meeting in five minutes. Bring your food, you can eat there."

With that he wandered away, aimless, like an old man overwhelmed by a fantastic flea market.

"Pancake's ready," she flipped it onto my plate with the motion of a professional chef. It didn't look like Bugs Bunny, just a formless blob that, with a fantastic imagination, sprouted some ears.

I hate the workings of the house. If I show them that I have my manic depression under control, they'll let me go home. All I have to do is play the game better than they do.

Princess was intently filing her nails and I just realized that I had never seen her without that nail file. I'm surprised they let her have one. Maybe like Reno she "graduated" to using sharp objects.

Big Daddy sat in the old Laz-E-Boy recliner that obviously had his name on it. It's the best seat in the house and no one even attempted to take it.

"Since we're all here, let's get started a little early so we can finish sooner. But first, to address Isaac's concerns about sleeping late. I've talked it over with Big Mama and we agreed to let you sleep until nine. I know that's not much longer, but it's better than nothing and these days you have to take what you can get. Now, what was particularly difficult to deal with this week?"

"I'm still feeling kind of guilty over breaking up with my girlfriend," Blaine said. "Her best friend sits across from me in Algebra class and she hounds me with these dirty looks. I try to figure, forget her, what does she know? But then I don't know. I still feel that I shouldn't have done it."

"Shouldn't have done it?" Reno's voice cried with indignation. "She was a slut. Sleeping around on you, and you feel guilty?"

"Reno, she wasn't a slut."

"Blaine, she was sex on wheels."

"Now, Reno, let's not resort to name calling. That never solves any problems and usually leaves a few broken feelings in its wake," Big Daddy's voice was calm, yet control leaked from it at every angle. "Blaine, it is perfectly natural when you have to do something unpleasant that you doubt yourself. The important thing is that you don't let it take its toll on your self-confidence. If the girl was not helping your psychological development, then perhaps what you did was the best thing to do."

"And my schizophrenia, I think she liked the attention she got from dating a 'crazy' guy. It's all we ever talked about."

Princess put down the file long enough to run her fingers through her hair. "At my school no one knows about my nervous condition, and no one ever will."

"At first, I told my close friends because, well, they are my close friends, I wanted them to know." Blaine was quick to defend himself. "Then I told my teachers to let them know why I missed all that time in September. From there, people just drew their own conclusions. I was acting pretty strange and it would be stupid to pretend that nothing was wrong. But I don't care who knows now. If they have a problem with it, then screw them."

"Well, that's one way of dealing with it. Does anyone have any other suggestions?"

"No, I'd say 'screw them all' is a pretty good philosophy," Isaac rebounded.

"Any suggestion we have for Blaine in dealing with his feelings?" Upon seeing no response, Big Daddy assigned Blaine duties to clean the downstairs bathrooms. It was important that the house look especially nice because today was the annual Parents' Day Grill.

"Grill?" I asked, my mouth full. "What grill?"

"Oh, Taylor, I forgot to mention it. This afternoon is our annual Parents' Day Grill. I mentioned it to your mother, but it was quite some time ago. After the meeting you may use the phone in my office to give her a call."

Their eyes burned into me. The phone in the office. It was obviously a privilege they'd never had. They hated me. Strike one in the balance for getting out of here.

"Isaac?"

"Pretty uneventful week. Still hot for the blonde."

"Have you asked her out?"

"No."

"Why not?"

"I just can't." Isaac's reply was sharp and penetrating. Big Daddy moved on.

"Reno, what are some of the things you've been dealing with this week?"

"I tell you, Big Daddy, you are just not going to believe it. I'm in history class and I get a call from, who else, the President of the United States. He tells me to come to Washington, but I told him we had the grill this weekend and I just couldn't leave town."

"How very thoughtful of you, Reno, I'm flattered. Has Maria started talking to you yet?"

For the first time I saw Reno's face fall, scraping the ground with resentment. He could play her like a Steinway.

"No. She hasn't talked to me since I was hospitalized in June. She looks down on me now, like I'm weak or I'm not as strong as she is. She hasn't told anyone, but I can tell she's hovering it over me, waiting to use it at just the right time. I should be like Blaine and not care who knows. I mean, everybody's got problems, why should we keep ours in the closet when other people can drag theirs out in broad daylight? I want to tell everybody why I went to the hospital just to beat her to the punch. But I can't do it."

"Does anyone have any suggestions on how Reno should deal with this problem?"

"I say you have better friends than that in this very room," Blaine reached over and rubbed her shoulder.

"We all know you're the best, Reno," Isaac added.

I thought the thing was starting to get all warm and fuzzy and then Big Daddy barked out the chores.

"Reno, upstairs bathrooms, living room. So, Taylor, do you have anything you would like to share with us?"

"Not really."

"Aw, sure you do," Reno grabbed me into a headlock and started rubbing her knuckles on my head. "Tell them about that Bugs Bunny pancake I made for you this morning."

"Yeah, Reno made me a Bugs Bunny pancake this morning." I hoped she'd let go.

"Made extra special just for you."

"Made extra special just for me." She let go.

"You mean you aren't dealing with any issues right now, Taylor?" Big Daddy knew I was struggling and was trying to get me to spill my guts.

"I guess the main thing is just dealing with being here. I'm not too crazy about it."

"Most people aren't wild about Saint Jude's when they first arrive here. But you'll adjust. We're like an extended family. Taylor, please clean the kitchen and wash dishes." With a flick of his index finger, he motioned for me to follow him.

It was better to be in Big Daddy's office for a purpose other than talking to him. It took all the edge off, erased the feelings of guilt that emerged from God only knows where. His phone was cold and heavy. The speaker end of the receiver was dirty, and I made little marks in the dirt with my fingernails. I briefly debated whether or not I wanted to put it near my face.

"This is the Drysdale residence. We can't come to the phone right now."

She changed it.

Down receiver. Redial.

Busy signal.

That's not the message on the phone before I went to Brick House. Before it was, "Susan and Taylor can't come to the telephone . . ." She erased my name.

And we had such fun making it, too. We did it in different voices at first, pretending we were French, with party music playing in the background, or that we were Laverne and Shirley, Lucy and Ethel, Thelma and Louise. But we had to stick with a boring message just in case someone from the office called. But even with that "serious" message, our minds were so full of laughter, we had to redo it four times. Even still, if you listened carefully, you could hear me stifle a snicker when saying my name.

Redial. Third ring.

"This is the Drysdale residence. We can't come . . ."

Rewritten. Erased from my own home.

". . . a message, we'll get back to you as soon as possible."

"Mom, it's me. There's a barbecue thing going on here at Brick House. Anyway, it's for all the parents. Thought you'd like to come. It's around fourish if you can. Bye."

I wanted to say something about changing the message, but the words wouldn't come. After all, it was all technically hers, the answering machine, the house, the phone . . . but I wanted to ask her why I had been evicted.

I stayed on the line until the answering machine hung up on me.

The road to the kitchen seemed a mile long and fifty miles wide, with the walls backing away from me, afraid to touch me. The way my classmates would react if word ever got out that I was here.

Chapter 5

You will be assigned hours, or certain chores to perform on a daily basis. Failure to do these tasks in a timely fashion will result in a loss of privileges . . .

The dishes were plain and plastic and if I used my imagination just right, I could still picture the Ingle's $1.99 sticker in construction orange glaring at me from the suds. There were some bright yellow rubber gloves beside the sink, but I didn't see them until after I stuck my whole hands ruthlessly into the water.

From the sink the window provided a view of the front yard and Epson Street. 155 Epson Street.

You hear things. Floating out from under a bathroom stall or snippets of careless conversation whispered too loudly on the phone. That's where you hear rumors about Brick House. No evidence to substantiate them, just words lofting by on the cloud of conversation, becoming more solid with every spoken word until, bang, they knock you down with a force so great, you wonder how you could've mistaken it for something light and lofty.

I had heard things.

At Brick House, the first thing you underwent was a detoxification. They lock you in a rubber room for twenty-four hours and watch to see how weird you get. They don't let you go to the bathroom, either.

Everyone at Brick House was a violent criminal.

The psychiatrist just wants to get you into a period of dependency, so he can seduce the young girls. The psychiatrist, you see, was an old man, and he liked them young.

No one stops by there trick-or-treating since a young boy found a razor blade in his apple. They were going to file a lawsuit, but they got threats from the two residents accused of manslaughter and dropped the suit.

It doesn't take much for rumors to solidify into fact. All it takes is the watering of lips and firm jaws, a command of the English language that would have made even Shakespeare proud. And it takes a soul that's not afraid of taking the truth and trimming it into a work to call its own. It was an art form, really, rumor-making was. And all the masters of that art are at my school.

I felt something smooth and sharp in the dishwasher. Gingerly, I wrapped my fingers around the object and pulled out a sharp knife. A mistake. Weren't these things supposed to be locked up?

Mom kept me away from knives ever since I was stood up by David.

He was really a wonderful guy. I know he only did it out of ignorance and intolerance. After all, he was four years older than I. Could you really expect a senior to be tolerant of the actions of a freshman?

He didn't say much to me after we had a disastrous date at the state fair. He didn't understand. He didn't understand that the world was bright that day, and he should have rejoiced in it with me.

After the state fair episode, he avoided me. He went to class by walking on the outside of the building to avoid me in the halls—even in the rain. And the notes left in my locker? That stopped abruptly. Finally, one day I confronted him and asked him if we were going to go out again or were we just finished. I just wanted a straight answer. I even phrased it in a yes or no question.

He hemmed and hawed, picking at his peach fuzz mustache until he muttered he'd meet me at the drive-in on Friday. There was a double feature, he said.

I said I would be there at eight. He nodded. I know that he nodded. It was confirmed. He would deny it later, but I saw the bob of the head. Up. Down. Yes.

I got Patricia to take me there, like I got her to take me everywhere. David was a senior and, as my mother said, had no business robbing the cradle unless he was trying to rob me of something else.

The drive-in was closed. Patricia told me it had been closed for a month now.

Patricia wanted to leave right then, but I insisted that we wait, which we did for about a half hour. Then Patricia drove us away over my glaring protests.

"Taylor, he's not going to be here."

"He said he would."

"If I were you, I would pretend that we never even came here. We'll say that you saw right through him from the start. You don't need to have everybody know that you're a freak."

It was in the way she said it. "You're a freak." So plain, so matter-of-factly that she might as well have said that the sky was blue.

But what hurt was that it came from her. David was the object of my desire, Patricia was the groundwork for my faith.

My fingers started to sting. I'm not sure where it came from, if it came from David or the fact that my voice was no longer on the answering machine.

I stared long and deep at the knife in a glare that took forever. Its smooth surface. The twisted reflections in its blade. The calm peace of the wooden handle.

Everyone knew I was a freak. Tears melted their way into the dishwater. People couldn't handle something different because it's too beautiful to look at, and it leaves them blind for an instant, blinking hard as if they've been looking at the sun.

After all, look what happened to Christ.

"Hey, Taylor, is something . . ." Big Daddy removed the knife from me before I knew he had entered the room.

"I just found it . . . in the dishwater."

"We'll just lock this away for now," he said.

My mind raced with words too quickly for me to express. Would that put me in the rubber room they're supposed to have here? Put me on surveillance?

"Taylor, why don't you go into my office and have a seat. I'll be there shortly. Reno can finish the dishes."

I could tell he was one of those who tried to be a fatherly presence but failed miserably. It was clear in his entire being. It was in his voice, the way it strained to keep from faltering or cracking. It was in the way his hands made awkward motions in the sky. It was in his begging eyes that seemed to scream, "I'm your best friend" a little too loudly.

He prattled on about how Saint Jude's was like a family, and how we should inform him if we have any problems or start to feel bad. It was obvious that he had given this speech so many times he was doing it by rote; all his hand motions were scripted and his body knew precisely at the right times when to jerk and groan.

Finally, it came.

"Taylor, why didn't you tell me that you found a knife?"

"It didn't seem important." I didn't want to tell him that I was too busy thinking of my tattered love life.

He held his hand up tentatively to silence me, like an awkward Moses at a Red Sea that appeared a lot bigger than he initially thought.

"Explanations aren't necessary. We'll go into explanations later. You used knives to cut yourself before, didn't you?"

Cat scratches. No big deal. It's not like I slit my wrists or anything. Mom found out and she went mental. Shipped me off to the crazy barn.

"Now, is your mother coming to the cookout?"

He was trying to change the subject to get me to relax.

"I couldn't reach her. She changed the answering machine," I blurted, finally.

"Changed it?"

"Yes," I hesitated. It all seemed so foolish now that I was explaining it to someone. "She took my name off the answering machine. She erased my message."

"Maybe it's hard for her to deal with not having you at home, and the answering machine just makes her realize how much she misses you."

It was a roundabout way of pinning a rose on something that stank.

"I almost forgot, your mother came by here this morning. I meant to ask her about the cookout then, but I was dictating some notes and forgot all about it."

"Why didn't you get me?"

"You were still sleeping. Yesterday was a rough day for you. We wanted to be sure you had plenty of rest. Anyway, she left something for you." He rose from his chair and with his key unlocked the closet.

Please God, let it be . . .

He pulled out my familiar friend. I could feel my lips curling into a smile. The reason: I saw the backstage pass stuck to the case.

"I talked to your mother about the security policy and when you're not playing it you may keep it in the locked closet. Only I have the key," he said. Then he leaned closer to me, as if we had achieved a new level of intimacy. "Tell you what, why don't you take the rest of the morning off and go play your guitar. Just be ready for the cookout this afternoon."

I nodded briskly. Anything to get out of his office.

Chapter 6

You are expected to attend all therapy sessions and Saint Jude functions. We expect that you will be honest and respectful of other members at all times. Staff may intervene and set limits if necessary . . .

They've decorated the house in such a God-awful way that it has to be a sin. The front porch has a large "Thou Shalt Not" sign hanging over it. Streamers hang loosely around the broken swing and the porch eaves, looking like a ticker tape parade gone awry.

Isaac made a makeshift sign that said "Saint Jude." Big Daddy was really pleased with it. It had an angel with wings and hands in the praying position—I assumed it was Saint Jude himself. But if you looked closely, you could see the fringes of a long devil's tail poking around the corner of the bottom of the robe.

Reno said Big Daddy was lucky that's all Isaac did. He had a taste for the morbid.

"He was one of those kids who pulled the wings off of flies," she said, as if that statement was all that was needed to explain Issac.

The parents had trickled in and were in the fenced back-yard like it was a PTA function. Big Daddy was at the grill, wearing an apron that said "Burnt is Beautiful."

I took my plate and retreated to the back porch, where I sat in a lawn chair that looked like it was hanging by a thread.

The inside of my burger was pink and made me sick to look at it, so I concentrated on the assortment of parents who had gathered around the picnic table. Reno's mother with her straight brown hair and retro wardrobe, looking like a hippie straight out of the Sixties. She didn't shave her legs, either.

"Pardon me, madam, is this seat taken?" It was Blaine.

"Go ahead."

Sitting beside a guy does something strange to me. It reminds me of David and the drive-in movie, of all the times I've been left behind.

"Is that Deana's dad?" I asked. He was the only one in a suit and looked like he came straight from the office, even though this was Saturday.

"Yep."

Deana and her father were almost posed, like department store mannequins that had just gotten makeup and clothes right and were now afraid to move.

Isaac and his mom—a short, overweight blonde—were talking to Big Daddy. I was too far away to make out what they were saying, but I noticed Isaac's mom wringing her hands and shaking her head a lot. Then—and I swear she really did this— she took a Kleenex from her purse, blotted it in her mouth, and wiped parts of Isaac's face.

"Poor guy, gotta feel for him," Blaine said, realizing that we were watching the same thing. "Look around at them. They are the reasons that we are the way we are. Or at least, that's what we'd like to think. Trigger wishing, I call it."

"What?"

"Trigger wishing. Its like how sometimes you get so frustrated that the blame has to come out some way. So you take your trigger finger, point it at the nearest target—usually your parents—and say bang! That's why I am the way I am.' "

"I guess."

"Man, I would hate to be a parent. I mean, one slip up in toilet training and your kid is messed up or worse."

"Somehow, I don't think it's that simple."

"It never is, doll, it never is."

For some reason, I didn't mind him calling me "doll."

"So, Taylor, what do you think of Brick House?"

"I think it stinks."

"I did, too, at first. Ran away twice. But you'll get used to it. It isn't all that bad. Think you'll call it home?'

"I'm getting out of here as soon as possible."

"That's what I said, too. You know, you are one good actress."

"What do you mean?"

"The way you go along with Reno's games. You sense that she's in charge and you kowtow to her."

"You're being ridiculous," I turned my attention to my pink burger.

"No, no, I mean it as a compliment. Means you're clever. You're a survivor. With a mental illness, you've got to be."

"Look, I don't care how long you and company have been here, I'm leaving soon."

"Shame," he said, taking a bite out of his pickle. "You're kinda cute."

I knew he couldn't have been talking about me, with my tomboy figure and stringy dishwater blonde hair. I glared at him skeptically. He winked.

"Taylor," Big Daddy called. "Why not take your guitar and provide us with some entertainment?"

I put down my food and opened up the case. She was a real beauty, with pearl inlay between the frets and a highly polished wood finish. I take my place in front of them and they stare at me hungrily. Reno lets out a few cat calls, as if she were my own personal agent, and I'm suspicious that she had a hand in getting Big Daddy to ask me to perform.

"Taylor, how about playing a song that you wrote?" Big Daddy asked.

I rarely perform my own work in publc. Mainly because

I'm afraid it'd be like watching other folks' home movies—
something that bores you to tears but you're too polite to say
anything. I only performed one other time, at a local beatnik
coffee house during open mike night, but most of the clientele
were stoned or asleep, and my performance only brought sparse
applause, amid a din of conversation and rattling dishes.

My voice, a grainy alto, gingerly sang:

"Laughing is hollow at the corner of my mind,
Laughing at me because you left me behind.
Forgotten from the world that was you,
In someone I can hold,
Maybe there's a place for me, too . . ."

At first when I finished, they just stared at me, as if they were
amazed that such a song could come from an ugly duckling
like myself. Eventually, applause scattered and grew.

"Yeah," Reno squealed between whistles. "Where did you
learn to play like that?"

"I think we have our entry in the church talent show this
year," Big Daddy patted me on the shoulder, smiling.

After the spotlight grew dim and I weaved my way back
to the porch, Blaine came jogging over to me.

"That was great—you were great!" The boyish sparkle in
his eyes was so bright this time that it focused all my attention. "And you wrote that?"

"Yeah. I got it in my head during a layover at the Charlotte
airport. I hummed the tune all the way on the flight home so
I wouldn't forget it."

"You've got talent. I heard you playing in your room earlier today, but you were just messing around. Have you ever
performed for anyone?"

"Just a few open mike nights. Mom doesn't let me do very
many of them."

"Why?"

"Because usually college kids are there and they've been drinking and—"

"Mommy doesn't want her little baby to be swept off her feet by some big man on campus."

"She's been very overprotective ever since Kaye died."

"Kaye?"

"My sister. She died in a car crash."

"Sorry . . . hey, why don't you strum a few more chords on that thing?"

"Sorry," I placed it back in its case, "the performance for this afternoon is over."

"Did I tell you about my musical career?"

"No."

"Played trumpet in the sixth grade. Quit band, though."

"Why?"

"The other kids made fun of me. Said it was a sissy thing to do. And at the time in band we were playing things like 'Mary Had a Little Lamb,' so I didn't really have a good argument against them. But, boy, I loved that trumpet."

"It's always good to meet a music lover."

"Music? I meant as a weapon. One day after school, those bullies came to me and just *wham*! Upside their head with the trumpet case. It was the most rewarding experience I've ever had, musically."

"I'm bored."

"They're serving some of Big Mama's blueberry pie."

"I don't feel like dessert."

"I know. It makes you sick just to look at them. A bunch of stuffed shirts pretending they're having a good time. Except Reno and her mom. I think they must've smoked something before they came."

I nodded.

"Hey, wait a minute. I've got just the thing." He disappeared into the storage shed and returned with a volleyball.

"Wait, I'm a musician, not an athlete."

"We'll trade. You teach me to play guitar, and I'll teach you how to spike a few."

He sets the shot and I take it. I miss the first two. The third time I hit it, but I miscued and my fingers only gave a soft tap to its leather surface.

"No, it's more like this," and Blaine threw the ball in the air and pounded a few into the ground. "Your turn."

"I'm afraid you've got an uphill battle before you." This was getting embarrassing.

"Rome wasn't built in a day," he replied, undaunted. "Wait a minute . . " There was that gleam in his eye, twitched with a hint of mischief. "Set it up for me. Watch this."

I did. He quickly looked around and he spiked it right into Princess' arms, spilling her pie all over her new dress. I was relieved that this was all the damage it did, since at first the ball was heading for her face. Princess was furious. Her face was a portrait of indignation etched in stone. Her mouth curled in such a horrible scowl I doubted if even the Medusa could come up with one that menacing.

"Blaine! Taylor!" It was Big Daddy. I was surprised to hear my name included. He marched over to us, a stiff, steaming battle sergeant. "What do you think you're doing?" He hissed.

"It was an accident," Blaine pleaded.

"Accident my ass," he said with biting calm and clarity, but softly, so the parents wouldn't hear him. "You're both in big trouble. See me immediately after the picnic."

When Big Daddy retreated, Blaine broke into a smile. "It was worth it, wasn't it?"

How could I tell him? How could I call him a fool because he didn't realize that these antics were only forcing me to stay at Brick House another day longer. This would go into my file and come up whenever I asked for leave privileges.

*   *   *   *   *   *

After a long lecture by Big Daddy, we were given the dubious honor of cleaning up after the picnic. Tattered paper plates and Styrofoam cups with little teeth marks around the rim littered the tables. I stuffed them into the Hefty bag like I was stuffing them down Blaine's throat. I hoped he noticed. Crunch. Pretty boy brat. Why did he have to drag me down into his private hell? Sure, he disliked Princess—as did half the Free World, obviously—but he didn't have to include me in on his assassination plots.

"You're upset, aren't you?" Blaine said as he rolled up the paper tablecloth.

"Really? Does it show?" My best sarcastic voice.

"I know what's upsetting you, but don't feel bad about it. I know where you're coming from."

Was that the hint of an apology?

"Taylor, my mom didn't show up, either. They don't like to come to Brick House often. It only reminds them that they no longer have me under their little thumb. They can't handle that. Why didn't your mom come?"

"I . . ." Gotta come up with something. Gotta sound good. "She had to go out of town. I didn't know about the cookout until after she had left. She would've come, I know. She loves this place, to hear her talk about it . . ."

"Don't make excuses for her, Taylor. That's the first thing you've got to learn if you're going to survive at Brick House. No excuses. Sure, it would be nice if we could all blame it on an old girlfriend, whatever, but in the end, shifting blame doesn't heal and it only locks you deeper into Brick House.'

"I won't be here long."

"You'll be here forever if you don't listen to me."

"So when did you become an authority? You're still here."

"I'm here because I want to be."

"You want to be here? You really are nuts."

Blaine sighed and plopped into a lawn chair, Hefty bag by his side.

"Taylor, I have a confession to make. I pull little stunts just to be sure I don't get out. Like that thing with Princess I just did? All planned."

"Well, I want to get out of here, so don't include me in any more of your plans."

"I just don't want to go home."

"Why would you rather stay here?"

"You don't know what it's like at my home. The shouting—Lord, the constant shouting. Everything becomes a major issue. Mom and Dad, making their children miserable, but they won't get a divorce because they're super-religious and believe that's wrong. So instead of everybody just going on with their lives, they instead have to torture both themselves and us for God knows how long."

"Well, I guess it stinks to be you."

"You wouldn't be so sarcastic if it happened to you."

"Look, can we just finish with this so we can get out of here?"

"And do what?" He slowly rose from the chair. "We leave here and we do what? There's nothing else to do except let Big Daddy psychoanalyze you."

I said nothing and stuffed the last of the paper plates into the trash.

"At least you have your guitar. At least you have something you're good at. You have somewhere that you can hide. You're a musician."

"I thought I was a crazy musician."

"But it's cool for musicians to be crazy. This can be your mask. Somewhere to hide behind when things get a little too rough. A haven."

"You have one, too."

"No, I don't. That's why I'm still at Brick House."

"I can't believe you really like this place."

"It's a lot better than the real world."

Chapter 7

All visitors must be approved beforehand. Dates will be chaperoned until we are certain of your stability. Guests are not allowed in bedrooms . . .

I knew I would be the topic of the Castaways meeting that night, so I waited by my door for their familiar voices to fill the hallway. I waited forever, but the voices never came. The only voices were the ones that rattled in my head, softly at first, but then building to a darkened groan of malcontent. Whisperings of vague, forgotten mistakes. It's as if something's wrong with my soul; I turn open only empty longings to become someone else. Blaine said my music was a mask. But even at that you can't wear a mask all the time. It makes it very difficult to breathe.

I heard giggles coming from Reno's room. Her door was shut, and I wondered if Big Mama ever checked the doors after lights out.

I gently rapped on her door.

"Big Mama!" Muffled shuffling came from inside the room.

"I's me," I decided I'd better calm the panic.

"Who's me?"

"Taylor."

The door flung wide.

"Taylor! Come on in!" Reno was wearing blue jeans and a navy T-shirt, unbuttoned halfway to reveal the black lace bra underneath. Some guy was sitting on her bed with his shirt off.

He's drinking something, and through I can't see the label, I
think it's a Coors. He has long, dark curls and an Opie Taylor
face. He cautiously glanced at me.

"I'm sorry, I didn't know I was interrupting—"

"Nothing, you're not interrupting nothing, is she?"

"Speak for yourself," he said,as he finished the drink and
then crushed the can on his head.

"Tim and I were just getting in a little oo-la-la before I
go to confession on Sunday. I try to fit all my sin in on Saturday night, if I can help it. So what's up?"

"The volleyball. . . and Princess . . ."

"You sure did put a shine on Big Daddy's head with that
one. In front of the parents, too."

"It wasn't me, it was Blaine—"

"But it was good for you. Means you've got moxie. Heard
of that? Neat word, isn't it? Mox-ie!"

"But I don't want moxie." My voice sounded more whiny
than I intended. "I want to go home."

"Taylor, let's you and me have a talk." She pulled me over
to her bed and we sat down, Tim laid back to make room for
us. Reno slouched over and propped her elbows on his chest.

"How long have you been dating?"

They laugh.

"Well, if you can call this dating. Not a word about this
to anyone. Not even Blaine knows. If Princess caught wind of
it, she'd go straight to Big Daddy. It's just that, if I don't get
a little loving here and there, I'll go nuts. You know what it's
like. You've had a boyfriend, haven't you?"

She prattled for a while about how she met Tim. It took
me back to the last date I had, which was my freshman year.
Dave took me to the state fair.

I met him at the drug store. I had told Mom I was meeting Patricia. She wouldn't let me go out with Dave because
I was a freshman and he was a senior. We rode the rides and
ate, but I should have left before we went to the petting barn.

There was this kid, you see. He couldn't have been more than five. He was old enough to know better. We were at the petting barn where the chicks were kept. I heard a chick crying and there's this kid holding it tightly in his hand. He's so stupid he can't see that the chick can't breathe. Its spindly legs thrashed wildly and its eyes were starting to bulge. I told him to let it go, but he ignored me, all the time squeezing tighter.

My hand sprung out and slapped the kid upside his head. Any idiot could see it was time to let go. The mother came over and cussed me for all that I was worth, but I didn't hear her. I was looking at the chick. Dave had to pull me away.

I don't remember much else except the fireworks. We were in the parking lot, lying on the hood of his Mustang as the pools of light flooded our horizon. The whole world was gone.

As the lights exploded, it was like a part of me went with them. I danced on the hood of his car. I was exploding with joy. It was as if euphoria became my soul and the world was at my feet. I had fallen to the earth and burned as a bright comet. I danced on the car next to us, and the next, and the next. I had to touch everything with my light, my glory.

I didn't like the way Dave talked about it. As he told the story, it made me sound whacko and warped. He didn't understand it was a piece of glory. Like God had touched me that day and inspired me. But like the fireworks, I had burned too brightly and had been quickly extingusihed before falling to earth too soon.

"Yo, Taylor," Reno waved her hand in front of my face.
"Sorry."

"But as I was saying, Tim's dad owns O & B Construction Company. You know them. They built the houses next to Stonybrook. The nice houses."

"How do you get in here?" I asked Tim.

"I'm spry," his lips parted in a broad grin.

"He comes up the tree that's near my window."

I looked out the window, but the tree scarcely looked big

enough to hold a cat, let alone Tim. Maybe he was an angel. Maybe he just magically floated down and gave kisses to whoever was aching or feeling lonely. The angel of Saint Jude's. I figured I could at least write a song about him.

"First of all, Taylor, let me tell you that if you keep up that junk about going home, you're only going to drive yourself crazy . . . er . . . crazier."

"I can't help it. I hate this place."

"Hate? Whoa, whoa, now you're just whining."

"So why do you stay here? Blaine stays here because he hates his parents. Why are you here?"

"I'm here because I can get away with murder." She gave Tim a wet, sloppy kiss on the cheek. "Big Daddy thinks these are the days when kids shoot marbles and watch *Howdy Doody.* And Big Mama? As long as you don't bother her, she doesn't care."

"So you're here just so you can raise hell?"

"Sometimes, Taylor, I like to think of myself as someone else. I think I was conceived at Woodstock—yeah, I know that doesn't work out agewise but it's my fantasy and I'll live it out as I please—conceived at Woodstock, grew up in Virginia, because we all know that all the truly wealthy Southerners are from Virginia. I would go to school in Kentucky, vacation in Myrtle Beach, and visit my boyfriend at Chapel Hill. Nice life, isn't it?"

"Yeah, if we could all choose our lives like that."

"Why don't you? Go ahead."

"No."

"Taylor, better think about it. Because when push comes to shove you're going to need somewhere to hide, and it's a lot better if that somewhere is a world you made rather than one made for you."

"Well, in my world, I don't have this stupid illness."

"Look at it this way: all the famous people were really crazy. Well, since we're crazy, we're already halfway to fame."

"Who wants it?"

"You do. You want it bad."

"And how can you tell."

"Sixth sense."

Tim's fingers were nimbly nibbling at her elbow, and I could tell they had the appetite to go to other places. Time to exit.

"Let me know when you have another Castaway meeting."

"Won't hold one without you"

I leave, but out of the corner of my eye I saw Tim reach over and fumble with the buttons on Reno's blouse. I couldn't sleep the rest of the night for wondering what was taking place down the hall.

Chapter 8

At Saint Jude's, we recognize that you have spiritual needs as well as psychological needs. On Sundays we offer the option of attending the local Catholic church for Mass . . .

I decided to go to church to earn brownie points with Big Daddy. Also because Blaine refused to go, and I wanted to do something to separate myself from him as soon as possible. I was afraid I was underdressed until I saw Reno come down the steps in a T-shirt and torn blue jeans. Big Daddy wore a double-breasted suit that made him look like a TV lawyer.

The church was Our Lady of the Mountains, and it had a reputation for being a fairly wealthy church; parishioners comprised of doctors, lawyers and CPAs. Community notables had their children baptized there. The local newspaper publisher, the DA, and president of the Kiwanis went there.

Of course, we weren't required to go to church as a group; that would be guilt by association. We might as well wear a neon sign on our head saying, "We're crazy, we're at Saint Jude's." But I felt that I needed to be with Reno.

"Reno, for the love of Mary, you're not going to wear that, are you?" Big Daddy's voice was calm, dry.

"Man looks on the outward appearance, God looks upon the heart," Reno replied.

"I know you have nicer things to wear than that."

"God doesn't care what I wear. Why should you?"

"Well, I will at least insist that you change into a pair of blue jeans without holes ripped in them."

Compromise. Reno went upstairs to change.

Princess saunters down the stairs and she is dressed to the hilt. She has this hat-and-veil number that makes her look like a widow. I can't stand how she gets all that confidence from expensive clothes. It's as if they mold around her figure and produce an invisible force that pulsates through her arms and down into her legs.

"Big Daddy!" Blaine stamped down the hall, wearing only boxers. They were red and white and had small gray whales on them.

"Blaine! You are inappropriately dressed. Get back to your room and put on some clothes this instant."

"He trashed my room! The sorry bastard trashed my room!"

"When did this happen?"

"This morning! When I was in the bathroom. Trashed my posters!"

"We are headed to church right now, but we will deal with it when we get home."

"We will deal with it now!" Blaine said. "This is the third time it's happened this month. Either you deal with it or I start beating him."

"You will not be beating anyone."

"When is it going to stop?"

Just then Reno came down the stairs in her best blue jeans. Her bright eyes darted anxiously from Blaine to Big Daddy, even studying the matted air that hovered between them as a thick fog.

"When Isaac gets adjusted to his medication . . ."

"I don't care about his medication."

"Calm down, Blaine," Reno interjected.

"Stay out of this, Reno."

"Isaac's trashed my room before, too."

"You haven't had it happen three times in the last month. Well, Big Daddy, what are we going to do about it?"

"Why don't you just lock the door?" I said. Everybody was overlooking the simple solution.

Silence blasted me in the face like the icy fingers of an arctic night.

"Lock our doors. Why didn't I think about that?" Blaine's sarcasm dug deep. "Our doors don't lock, you idiot! Haven't you noticed that?"

"Blaine. I will give you to the count of five to go back into that room, get dressed, and calm down," Big Daddy said. "If you don't, I will assign you so many hours that only the Second Coming will pull you out from under. I don't like treating you like a child, but when you act like a child, you leave me no choice."

For a while, Blaine just stared at the floor, his right hand pulling at the sparse hairs on his chest. Then silently, he backed away; the boxer who blinked.

"Now," Big Daddy took a deep breath, as if he had not been breathing during that entire exchange with Blaine. "I was glad when they said to me, 'let us go into the house of the Lord.'"

The way I see it, Jesus had a girlfriend, only she's never mentioned in the Bible. She was his childhood sweetheart when he was growing up down at the carpenter's shop in Nazareth. Then just when they got old enough to get married, Jesus starts on this mission kick. He takes off to be baptized by a man who eats locusts (I never could get past that part) and takes off to the wilderness to torture himself. He leaves her behind.

That about sums up my relationship with Jesus. Sure, I knew He was there, but my Bible Belt upbringing made me believe that Jesus was like one of those really pretty dolls you just put on the shelf and never play with. To be human, it seemed, would be beneath Him

The service was like one of those minuet dances you read about in cultural history classes.

The brief sermon was on demons and the story about how Jesus healed the man with a demon and drove the demons into the pigs. He asked what were the demons we struggled with today.

I was always worried that Patricia was going to tell Nell about my manic depression. Patricia can handle the fact that she has a friend with a psychiatric file—after all, her dad is a recovering alcoholic, so she can't throw stones. But Nell—she was Free Will Baptist. I never knew much about the Free Wills except my mom told me that the girls weren't allowed to wear pants. Nell and I took a psychology class together. She said she thought that people who were mentally ill just really had demons in them, and she knew a deacon in Charlotte who could get rid of them by laying on hands. Was my problem that simple? Was there just a demon in me? I used to believe it was a punishment for something I did in a past life. Now I believe it's a punishment for just living.

Reno started whispering something in my ear. Her words were rapid and wispy so I had to ask her to repeat it.

"We're going to see Inez after church today."

"Who's Inez?"

"Who's Inez?" she said it so loud I thought the priest would hear. "She's only the best. She makes this fried chicken that's so—and biscuits with—oh, and fresh veggies from her garden."

"Shh." Big Daddy gave her a prod with his index finger. He was sitting behind her.

"I tell you, Inez is the best, she is just the best. Everyone should have a friend like Inez."

"Reno, would you please be—" Big Daddy was cut off in mid-sentence. Time for singing. But I can feel his eyes burning a small hole in the back of my neck.

*   *   *   *   *   *

Inez was a thin, petite woman with a thick mass of short, curly gray hair. Her sculpted cheekbones framed deep eyes and a wishful mouth. Reno ran up to her and grabbed her after the service, nearly knocking her to the floor. But Inez took it in stride, acting like a mother supervising her kids after a Christmas morning that was a little too exciting.

"Reno, you look well. Is the medicine helping?"

"I'm doing a lot better," she shrugged. "And this—" she grabbed me by the elbows and forced me into the front of the stage—"this is Taylor. She's new."

"It's nice to meet you, Taylor." Inez gave a smile that revealed perfectly straight teeth.

I forced out a grin, but only because I was biting my tongue at the same time.

"Do you have fried okra ready for us?"

"Yes."

Reno reached out with another hug, in a way that I never saw her share with her mother at the cookout.

Inez was within walking distance from the church, and her house was full of Native American artwork, ranging from elaborate bead jewelry to ceremonial mandalas. Reno whispered to me that Inez had done most of the artwork herself, that she taught Native American history at the local private college, and she was always the one quoted in the paper when they did articles about gambling being allowed on the reservation.

"My aunt was manic-depressive," Inez volunteered while helping Reno set the table. "She only knew peace the last ten years of her life, when they finally realized what it was. When I was a little girl, she used to scare me, but eventually I learned it was because she was sick, and she couldn't help it."

"Inez has been a great supporter of Saint Jude," said Big Daddy, leaning over to give her a hug.

The food was good. Reno wasn't exaggerating, but during dinner Inez did something strange to me. She took my hand and placed her other hand on my shoulder, right between the main course and strawberry shortcake.

"I want you to listen to what I tell you," she said. "Everybody has a cross to bear. So bear yours gladly. There are other crosses that are heavier, that may be covered with thorns, and yours, though it is large, it is smooth and you have your sisters to help you pick out the splinters, if there are any."

Strawberry shortcake was usually my favorite dessert, but it tasted bland and pointless. Reno smiled at me across the table and gleamed at me as though I had been handed the secret to life.

By the time we got to Saint Jude's, the storm with Blaine had long since passed. He scratched up a couple of Isaac's CDs, so he felt vindicated. Big Mama didn't find out until after the fact and waited for Big Daddy to get home before she did anything. Big Daddy assigned him ten hours of bathroom cleaning. That's why the toilets at Saint Jude sparkle like jewels.

Chapter 9

You will be expected to attend school regularly just as you would if you were at your home. Any sickness must be verified by a doctor.

I dreaded Monday worse than a root canal or final exam. Only Patricia knew that I was at Brick House, but I knew that somehow, news would leak out. It always did. Like about Lizzie when she was with that forty-year-old man and had to get an abortion. Nobody talked about it, no one said anything to her, but it was there, vaguely hanging in the air like icy fingers.

Big Mama made eggs for breakfast and asked me if I bought or brought my lunch. I said it didn't matter. She said Mom had left some money in my account at the home so I could buy pizza from the cafeteria if I wanted. I agreed because I had the impression that she didn't want to bother with making my lunch.

The bus didn't come to Brick House. That would be asking for ridicule. Big Mama took us to school while Big Daddy supposedly dictated notes in his back office.

Big Mama drove a blue Dodge minivan; the inside reeked of cheesy pine-scented air fresheners. She dropped Blaine off first, who was already running a little bit behind because he forgot to take the garbage out last night and Big Daddy made him take it out this morning. We had to get a fairly early start because only Blaine and Isaac went to the same high school. I went to Eastridge and Reno went to Clyde.

Reno was unusually quiet, and it made me wonder if she had planted a practical joke somewhere. Before she got out to go to school, she turned to me with a wink.

"Don't let them see your weak spots, because they'll go after them," she said.

"Now what was that all about?" Big Mama asked after Reno got out.

"Beats me." I sank deeper into the seat, planning that as soon as I got to school, I was going to walk home. It'd take me a good couple of hours, but it was definitely doable. Mom wouldn't be at home, so I'd have to use the key that is hidden in the plastic rock in the flower bed. I'll pop in a video, fix a ham and cheese sandwich and have supper ready and waiting for her when she gets home. When she sees how unhappy I am, how Brick House is making me worse, then she'll take me home. I'll get a job to pay back the deposit. Then we'll continue a tradition by fixing hot chocolate and watching James Bond films. Something we haven't done since Dad left.

Even as a little girl, I remember Dad as a strange one. Once he told me that Mickey Mouse lived in our chimney. At first I thought he was crazy, but now I realize he was just trying to get me to shut up about how I wanted to go to Disney World. I would hear their late-night arguments—frequently I got up to go to the bathroom and found Dad sleeping on the sofa.

I remember when I went to visit Leigh, who was in my kindergarten class. Her parents—who obviously never got the message that the honeymoon was supposed to be over—were cuddling in front of the TV, holding hands and occasionally kissing.

"Why are they doing that?" I asked.
"Because they're mommies and daddies. Mommies and daddies do that."

Well, right off I told her that I didn't know what kind of line they had been handing her, but I had a mommy and daddy and they definitely did not act like that.

Dad left silently. I just woke up one morning and he was gone. Mom spent that whole day in bed. I thought that she was crying, but she told me that she was sick and was about to throw up so I closed the door and left her alone.

At the front gate of school there was this huge metal lion— our mascot—decked in colors of red and gold. It's painted in such God-awful hues, you have to wonder how many cable channels the thing can pick up.

"Since I let you off last, I'll pick you up first," Big Mama said.

"Whatever."

"Don't make me wait. I don't want to come in after you."

"Don't worry, I don't want you to come in after me."

"Well, at least we agree on something. And smile, dear, it really does make you look prettier."

Suck it in your face. And I came very close to saying it.

In the hallways, cheerleaders worked on the banner for the spirit rally. They hated me because I didn't have designer jeans or fancy clothes. Actually I did have them. I'd go out and buy $500 worth at one time with Mom's credit card. But when I'd sober up I'd realize that I couldn't hide the credit card bill from her forever, and I simply took them back. Most of the time I never even took the tag off them.

As I walked to homeroom, there was the same burning sensation I felt when Big Daddy stared down the back of me and Reno in church. They knew. They knew all about me. They had read my thoughts.

I hung on every word they said, analyzing it and tossing it from side to side in my head. I opened my locker. It took me twice to do it because my hands were shaking.

"What'd you do this weekend?" It was Alan. His locker was beside mine.

Spent a weekend in hell, I felt like saying, but didn't.

"We tried to call you to go to a movie, but all we got was your machine."

Yeah, you and me both.

"Taylor? You okay?"

"Yeah. It's just a Monday."

"I know the feeling. Rumor has it we've got a pop quiz in algebra."

He knew about Brick House. It was like when you were little, and you knew that when your dad got home you'd get a spanking.

Through the day, the humming became louder. It was as if the whole classroom gave off this cosmic hum that emitted from their minds. It was soft at first, like the noise of an air conditioner. At first I thought it was the air conditioner, but it made no sense to have the air on in November. I realized it came from the class when Alan raised his hand to answer a question and the hum was louder than his voice.

This was supposed to be my best year. This was supposed to be the year when, as a senior, I get to relish the friends that I have built up over the last four years. Enter Brick House and it all goes up in smoke.

I excused myself to go to the bathroom. The teacher let me go because I rarely ask to venture into the stall sanctuary, littered with graffiti, cigarette smoke, and if the mood is right, a hint of marijuana.

My face in the mirror was strange and foreign. My eyes were sunken in, like the way you see heroin addicts. The reflection was cold and unforgiving. Lithium had helped some, but it made me thirsty and I had to pee all the time. My shrink said it wasn't so much finding the right medication as the right combination of medicines. That once it worked, all the tough times would be a memory. I would be perfect, like one of those big-breasted women you see in the Victoria's Secret catalog.

It came like a wave of nausea right before you vomit. It

was a mistake. I was the reason my parents got married, and what a rotten marriage they had. There was some talk of putting me up for adoption. I couldn't get past the fact that when my mother first found out that she was pregnant with me, her first thought was probably, "Oh, shit."

I was breathing in hot, erratic spurts. Warm tears poured down my cheek. The world was ending. Jesus said I was guilty. Heaven laughed at me.

I tried to turn the rage, looking for something to destroy as the burning got deeper and the humming started to hurt my ears. There was a paper towel dispenser hanging by only two screws. It came to the floor without much resistance. I tore one of the screws out of its home and plummeted the sharp end into my arm, just below the elbow. Judgment and doom subsided.

I was bleeding by the time the girl came into the bathroom. She came to pee, no way her fresh-as-apple-pie face could have smoked a cigarette or joint. She looked at me in puzzled confusion.

"What?" I mustered up the meanest voice I could find, but it ended up sounding hoarse and sick.

She backed away from the bathroom. I saw my reflection in her face. I was a dirty child with no way to go home.

Later, the same girl returned with the school nurse. She was obviously a freshman and didn't know any better. A senior would have left me alone.

"What seems to be the problem, Taylor?"

I started to reply but the tears got in my throat and I buried my head in my hands."

"Let's go lie down for awhile," she pulled the screw out of my hand and gave me some paper towels to stop the bleeding. It was my arm, and what I wanted to do with it was my own business. Nobody else's. No one.

The sick room smelled like that antiseptic spray they use at nursing homes. There was a small bed with an old, yellowed

comforter on it. Even the room looked contagious. I would probably come down with mono next week.

"Taylor, why were you hurting yourself?"

Most people didn't know about my being hospitalized. She
didn't, and I wasn't going to elaborate. I asked her if I could
go home.

"Certainly, I'll call your mother and have her come get you."

When Mom comes, she'll see how miserable I am at Brick
House. She'll see that I'm not any better, and then she'll have
to let me come home. I'll offer to fix supper so it'll be there
for her when she leaves the accounting firm. That's one thing
she always complained about: I never was much help around
the house. But that was mainly because I wasn't feeling well.
If she'd just let me come back home, I would feel better. Then
she'd see, supper would be ready, and we would be a family
again.

She said nothing when she came to pick me up, but there
were frustrated leers sparking out of her eyes. She didn't say
a word to me until we were on the expressway.

"Taylor, why in God's name—" then her voice broke off
with a strange little squeak. "I mean, why are you hurting yourself again? The cutting—I thought that you were past that now.
Isn't the medicine working?"

"It's Brick House. It makes me worse."

"It does not make you worse. You make yourself worse.
You're not trying hard enough."

"It's hard when you're trying all the time. I mean, no one
can try all the time."

She turned onto the wrong street.

"Mom, where are we going?"

"We're going right back to Saint Jude's."

"But you know how bad it makes me!"

"I can't leave you at home alone feeling like this, and I've
got to get back to work. Taylor, I can't come running from
work every time you decide to have a crisis."

"I didn't decide this, it just sort of happened."

"Well, your 'sort of happens' are becoming a lot more frequent. That's why you're in Saint Jude's."

"I don't like Saint Jude's. It reminds me of the hospital."

"Well, everything reminds us of something," and she bit her lip. I knew it was time to stop when she started biting her lip. Any argument now was moot.

When we pulled up to Brick House, the doors jeered at me. The front porch threatened to give way and swallow me whole.

Mom went inside and started explaining something to Big Mama. I just headed upstairs to my room. Moments later I saw her car pull away. Big Mama up the steps. Soft thuds. I counted them. Ten, eleven, twelve.

"Taylor?"

"I don't want to talk."

"Come down here and help me make some cookies."

"I don't want to."

"I didn't ask."

I followed her down to the kitchen, tail between my legs. Big Mama broke open one of those Pillsbury sticks of chocolate chip cookie dough and handed me a spoon and a cookie tray. A real spoon, too, not one of those plastic spoon/forks. I pinched out some of the dough for myself.

"The world is such a dark place," she said. "And most of the time, you keep fear of trying because you can't see. So we all got to hold hands. We're like children crossing the street, and things are flying at us so fast we can't keep up. We just hold onto each other."

My arm hurt. As if reading my thoughts, Big Mama asked me if I'd put peroxide on it. I told her the nurse did.

"You see, Taylor, it's not you that makes you do things like this. It's the darkness. A piece of it lurks in your mind, and sometimes you feel that you just have to let it out, or you'll bust."

Chapter 10

Everyone is expected to participate in group discussions. It is not fair to have unequal participation. We believe that the more you share with others, the more you will ultimately learn about yourself . . .

Days filtered in and out of Brick House like waiting for Christmas. You wait forever, but the closer it gets, the faster the days come, till they're hitting you, bam, bam, bam. Clinging for support. Darkness that weaved its way in and out of my mind like a fog.

My days were especially long since I was staying at Brick House now instead of going to school. I had a tutor and was given assignments, and Mom worked it out so it was similar to the system they had for kids who had to miss a lot of school because they got really sick from mono or something. She probably told my teachers about my "Condition."

"Don't blame yourself for the mental disorder. It is caused by a chemical imbalance, not something you did or said," Big Daddy would minister to us in group therapy sessions. Group therapy—that was a joke.

First of all, Isaac didn't want to talk about anything but sex, and whenever we commented he said that we all had penis envy. Frankly, I don't think Isaac meant a word of it, but he just liked being able to say the word "penis" in public and get away with it.

Blaine was supportive when I told them about school.

"You got to do what's best for you," he said. "I had a boss like that, didn't understand why I was having problems. He fired me. When I get out of this place and get a decent paying job, I'm going to hire a good a lawyer and sue his ass off for everything he owns."

"Blaine, weren't you fired for constantly coming to work late and leaving work early?" Big Daddy asked.

"That's beside the point, Big Daddy."

If I did learn one thing through group therapy, it was that my hospital experience was dramatically different from that of the others. Mom had good insurance, so she could afford to put me in New Way, the treatment program on the fourth floor of a private hospital in Asheville.

Isaac was sent to a state hospital. His stories often took up chunks of space in group therapy. How much was the truth and how much exaggeration, I couldn't tell.

"First, they herd you into this room like you're a bunch of cattle," he leaned to the edge of his chair. "The nurses are so busy with paper work, they can't watch you, which means that by the time they knew someone was attacking you, you'd be dead before they got there."

"What about the orderlies?"

"You got to watch out for them, they're all gay."

"Are not."

"All of them. Nurses, too."

"I don't believe a word of that," Reno said.

"My roommate caught two of them kissing."

"If they were Lesbians, they wouldn't be so open about it."

"I met this girl there, she claimed to have three tits."

"You're making this up."

"I saw it."

"What did you think?"

"Her breasts really weren't all that spectacular."

I never told my stories because they would pale by comparison. That's why I responded with "It was okay," when Big

Daddy asked me about my hospital experience. How could I tell him that there was ice cream behind the nurse's counter, and if you asked really, really, nice and didn't give them any trouble, that they would give you some? That we had cable TV and a VCR? How could I tell him that we had an art class where we made trivets and did paint-by-number?

And of course, the *Star Trek* story was definitely out.

A particularly suspenseful episode of *Star Trek* left me a little wired. I woke up that night screaming. I dreamed I was trapped in a small room with a dark looming evil like something from a horror movie. It was a spiritual manifestation of all that was demonic. It surrounded me in the room, choking me.

It wanted to possess me. It pressed about my face and tried to open my mouth and leap into my body. It had just reached out to consume me when I awoke screaming.

Instantly, a nurse was in the room.

"Are you all right?"

I told her it was just a nightmare, and I was sorry for disturbing her. She was a short plump woman with her graying hair tucked neatly in a hairnet that made her look like a cafeteria worker.

"There, there," she said, grabbing me by the neck and shoving my face in between her huge breasts. I nearly suffocated.

As far as psych wards went, I stayed at the Hilton.

Princess always smoked at group therapy, that is, whenever she showed up. Her complaints were petty, and amounted to little more than should she dump the guy she was dating because he had taken her out to the steakhouse instead of Deer Park Restaurant at Biltmore House. Big Daddy would just tell her to put out the cigarette. Sometimes she did, sometimes she didn't. It depended on what time of month it was.

I heard that Isaac was sexually molested by a sibling, male or female no one said. Someone noticed it when he began drawing odd pictures in his second grade art class.

They say the thing with Isaac is almost bizarre. It's like his mind switches to another track. He doesn't seem to know where he is or who he is. Everyone has seen this switch except me. No one likes to talk about it because, deep down, we're all afraid it will happen to us, and then we'll be wheeled to the state loony bin where they have the lesbian nurses and the three-breasted inmates.

Chapter 11

As a staff, we have a responsibility to provide an environment that is both safe and therapeutic. Your cooperation will make the environment better for everyone . . .

"Pity," Inez told me after church one Sunday morning, "is the car you ride in when you'd rather walk."

The urge to cut on myself still persists. In the meantime, I'm supposed to take something called Klonopin—it's basically like valium—whenever I get the urge to hurt myself.

Every day, Big Daddy checks my arms and legs to see if I've been cutting on myself, and Big Mama takes a quick glance at my body after I towel off from the shower.

"You're going down a road you do not want to go down," Big Daddy told me in my individual therapy session. "First, it's just your arms and legs, and then pretty soon, that's not enough. Then you have to cut on your face, stomach, breasts, and neck."

But they couldn't understand that it was like having a virus, and you had to throw up before you felt any better.

"Taylor, don't you see? You have the emotional pain and you are trying to have a physical pain to accompany it to give you some relief."

I didn't know how much of this psychobabble I wanted to buy into, but I guess it made sense at the time.

Blaine gave a peace offering to Princess and told her he would replace the blouse that he ruined with the volleyball episode. She just sniffed and told him he couldn't afford it.

Princess became even more hateful day after day. She would
sit and file her nails during group therapy sessions, a perma-
nent scowl etched across her face. She would put down whoever
was trying to open up to the group, and when it came her turn
she would complain that she would have to go to Atlanta to
get something to wear for the country club winter formal, because, God knows, you can't find anything suitable in Asheville.

It stings, and then sometimes it burns. It's when it burns
and stings that yesterday becomes a burden too sharp to bear,
and tomorrow becomes a twisted, warped reality. Mom never
understood this. "Why would anyone want to hurt themselves?"
she'd say. But she never felt the burning.

You can always tell people who feel the burning because
it's written in their eyes, the way the lids hang slightly heavier than normal, the way they casually forget the first names
of people they just met, the way their mind is enveloped in
a world that surrounds them like a liquor blender.

Blaine said it casually, almost as an afterthought.

"What are you doing tonight?"

"What everybody else is doing, movie night."

"Would you like to come with me to pick out the movie?
I've earned enough trust that Daddy W is letting me do it
unsupervised. Plus, he has a meeting early tomorrow with the
board of directors, so he'll be skipping out on the flick."

"How did I get this honor?"

"You're kinda cute."

"Says who?"

"The committee."

"There's a committee?"

"The 'Built Like a Brick House Committee.' They voted
you Queen of Brick House.'"

"Oh, now that's an accomplishment."

"Famous women have been Brick House alumni."

"Name one."

"Well, I can't name them. It's all very confidential you see. Hush, hush."

"I'm sure."

"Last year's Miss Brick House went on to star in several feature films."

"Okay, that's enough. How far are you going to go on?"

"Until I get you to go with me . . . until I get you to believe that you're pretty."

Pretty? What'd he know about pretty? Only *Playboy* magazines hidden under the mattresses, necking with the homecoming queen during half time. Not me. Not pale-faced, mousey-haired me, with the microscopic breasts and—thanks to Brick House's supervised shaving policy—hairy legs.

Big Mama drove us to the video store. Blaine sat behind me. I thought I felt his fingers dancing along my neck. Keep cool. Make sure it's what you think it is before you draw any conclusions. That's what Dave said, and that I had the mistaken belief that he liked me. Never mind that we held hands while we were on the ferris wheel.

The video store was behind a gas station and was one of those mom-and-pop varieties. The selection, Blaine told me, was horrible, but they let Brick House rent movies for free.

The whole place was falling apart. Movie posters were bent and frayed. A large glass concession stand offered some stale popcorn for sale, and a kid at the checkout counter, that I swear didn't look a day over twelve, was puffing away at a pack of Marlboros.

"Now don't take all day," Big Mama glanced at her watch. "Pick something tasteful. We've been very pleased with your selections so far."

"She trusts me," Blaine whispered as soon as we were out of earshot. "Time to move in for the kill."

The covers to the movies were worn at the edges. Blaine

explained to me that you didn't take the cover up to the counter and then get the movies, but that the movies were right there on the shelf, ready for the taking. As if they didn't have to worry about anyone stealing anything.

There was an R-rated foreign movie out entitled *The Traveling*. It played only in drive-in theaters, and it was supposedly based on a dirty book. Blaine wanted it because it was rumored that it had full frontal nudity.

He sneaked it off the shelf like a prime cat burglar.

"Now dig this." He whispered it so close to my ear that I felt his warm breath against my neck.

Blaine took a copy of *Bambi* and switched covers. Then he leaned over, as if to whisper something to me. He glanced over his shoulder to be sure Big Mama was out of view. I leaned forward. His lips grazed the top of my cheek. He pulled away and winked.

I was like a kid who didn't know which birthday present to open first. This could not be happening to me. I danced on cars, remember? I was the nutcase. The whacko. The wallflower no one wanted to dance with. The schizo. The psycho . . . the object of Blaine's affections.

So I guess it really could happen . . .

At Brick House, Blaine orchestrated the movie night like a well-oiled machine. He had programmed Reno to start choking on popcorn if nudity was on the screen and Big Mama was anywhere nearby. This would cause a distraction long enough for him to stop the movie.

"But what if she really thinks I'm choking and starts beating on my back?" Reno asked.

"You're a tough girl. I have confidence in you."

We all recognized, of course, that there was the possibility that Big Mama could actually really care less about what we put on the TV, but we felt it was better to go along with Blaine's plan, just in case.

Fortunately, Big Mama spent all her time in the kitchen.

Doing what, I wasn't sure, but no one cared to find out.

The movie had very little plot. Something about smuggling priceless works of art. The whole thing took place in France.

"You know this is going to be good," Blaine beamed. "I mean, France. That's where all the good skin flicks are from."

"You know they don't wear any clothes in France?" Isaac said. "It's like one big nudist colony."

"That's a bunch of crap. French people do wear clothes," Reno countered.

"Have you been there?"

"I've seen pictures."

"Those don't count. The French in the cities just put on clothes for the tourists. Out in the country they are naked."

A lot of things exploded in the film, but still, no nudity. The movie was winding down and the hero and heroine found themselves in a hotel room late at night.

"Here it comes!" Blaine tried to keep his voice down.

It was a love scene, but it was done in the dark, so you really couldn't tell what was what. After that, she got up to get a drink of water. In the bathroom light you briefly caught a glance of her breasts.

Then came the closing credits.

"That's it?!" Blaine squealed. "That's it?! I risked an extra three or four hours of chores for that? That's nothing. I mean, that could be shown on Saturday morning cartoons."

Reno stopped the tape and took it out of the player, examining the label.

"Your problem, dearest Blaine," she said, "is that you can't read. It says right here in small print: 'Edited Version.'"

"Censorship!" Blaine placed his hands on his temples and rolled on the floor.

Chapter 12

We encourage healthy relationships with your family members. Just because you are at Saint Jude does not mean that you are cut off from your family . . .

My Dad didn't do too much for me, or at least, that's what Mom always told me. But I knew it wasn't true. After all, Dad was the one who taught me how to fire a gun.

I was in seventh grade, and he and my cousin went down to my grandfather's barn to shoot holes through oil cans. My cousin had bought this fancy new automatic pistol that was from Russia. It had a big red star on the holster with the letters C.C.C.P.

They had been shooting at them for half an hour when curiosity pulled me toward them. What would happen if I got hit with a stray bullet? I focused on my body on the evening news with scads of reporters and photographers huddled around my family. Then they'd take my father and cousin off to jail, even though it was an accident, and they'd be in there for months before Mom could raise bail.

Daddy pulled me aside and showed me the gun.

"The most dangerous thing in the world," he said, "is a gun in the hands of someone who doesn't know how to use it. I hope you never have to know this, but I'm going to show you how to use a gun."

Gunpowder laced the air. The gun looked light, but it was heavier than I had imagined. The steel was cool and smooth. I wondered what it would feel like to have it pressing against my temple like you see in all those cop show dramas on TV.

He placed his stout figure firmly behind me, holding my arms as I fired. The shock knocked me back against his chest. In actuality, I probably missed all of the oil cans and hit the red clay bank. But I found a hole that I claimed was not there before and claimed it for my own. My Dad and cousin agreed without protest.

Mom was furious. How dare he let me handle a weapon at my young age? I could've hurt someone and then we would have been sued. Mom was obsessed with being sued. It was one of many fights that just replayed itself over and over again with several different variations. Mom and Dad were good to me and my sister—they were just horrible to each other.

We never went out to eat or to ball games or to the movies as a family. One parent would take me and Kaye to some event. It was as if the two of them didn't want to be seen out in public together. It was as if as long as they weren't seen in public they could make up this story about how wonderful their marriage was. Both were too proud to get a divorce for the longest time. Too proud to admit failure.

When Kaye died, he blamed Mom because she was driving. Although the truck jackknifed into Mom's lane, it was still her fault. That was when I first realized what a jerk he could be. He couldn't internalize his grief. He had to use it to thrash about at others.

After Kaye's death, he kind of lost it. She had been the joy of his heart, not me. I mean, he was good to me, but she was his princess. She was so beautiful, too, with dark raven strands of curly hair, a far cry from my dishwater blonde.

I had heard nothing from him since the divorce. He went to L.A. to head up this new recycling company. He didn't even ask if we wanted to go. He knew the North Carolina mountains were the perfect place to raise a family—not L.A., which is going to be the first thing burned off the map at the Second Coming. Who could blame him? We were in a small town outside of Asheville where people didn't even lock their cars.

The other day I got a postcard from him. It was mailed to Brick House. Daddy W looked at it skeptically before handing it to me, as if he wasn't sure I was ready to handle it. I love the way other people read your mail the first chance they get.

Thank God he didn't mention anything about my Condition on the postcard. I could just see every postman from here to L.A. wondering about this poor, crazy teen hick in Southern Appalachia.

Dear Taylor,

Your mom told me that you were sick. I hope you are feeling better. If there is anything I can do for you, don't hesitate to call me. My heart is with you.

Love,
Dad.

Mom wasn't too impressed with it. She just held it between her thumb and forefinger, flipping it from side to side as if it were some foreign object she had never seen before.

"Hmm," she muttered, trying to sound thoughtful. I could tell she was looking for a way to place fault, but she didn't.

"Your father," she sighed, "has a lot of problems."

And that was that.

Mom didn't come to see me at Brick House too often. I could tell it really bothered her. Maybe they told about the rubber room and she wondered if I had to be put in there. We didn't talk much. She didn't like to sit out on the front porch because she was ashamed to be seen with me.

It really burns when you feel you are a disgrace to your parents and there's nothing you can do. Even if they're lousy parents, they somehow hope that by making you, they can make

the world right and thus pay penance for all their past mistakes.
It's as if they've created this wonder child to carry their sins
all the way to Calvary—and further if needed.

I kept wanting to ask her about the erased message on the
answering machine, but I didn't have the guts. Besides, the answer was pretty obvious.

She wasn't just erasing me from the machine. She was erasing me from her life.

Chapter 13

Staying at Saint Jude's is not a right, it is a privilege. We reserve the right to revoke that privilege at any time if deemed necessary . . .

Even before group therapy I could tell Reno was about to blow. I had seen it in the way she scowled into her corn flakes that morning. I had no idea what was biting her, but I was afraid that asking would only make it worse.

Princess had sensed it and started picking at her. She had spent the night at Brick House because her father wouldn't let her go to Charlotte with a boyfriend. This, of course, flung her headfirst into an eruption of her "nervous condition," that Reno referred to as a load of crap.

In group therapy, Reno was spilling her guts about some friends at school that still did not want to associate with her since they found out that she was at Brick House.

"Now, are there any suggestions as for what Reno can do?" As usual, Big Daddy encouraged us to find our own solutions.

"Reno, man, I've told you and told you," Blaine rubbed his eyes, as if she were exhausting him, "Reno, forget those creeps. You don't need them. If they're going to turn their backs on you, then you're better off without them."

"Isaac?"

"Ditto," he made the peace sign. "More power to you."

"Deana?"

Princess fumbled in her purse for something, but apparently

never found what she was looking for. "Well, first . . ." and
here she let out a long sigh, as if simply breathing in Brick
House was enough to exhaust her, "First I would get rid of
that haircut and move on to something better. Preferably a cut
from this decade."

Reno exploded.

Within seconds she was on her feet. "You . . . you . . .
bitch!"

Each word was carefully formed, deliberate. Blaine jumped
and got behind her, ready to grab her hands if she made any
sudden moves toward Princess' throat.

"Now, Reno, try not to swear," Big Daddy gently corrected.

"And you," she turned on him. "You are even worse! I expect this kind of crap out of Princess, but out of you?"

"What do you mean?"

"What do I mean? The constant insults, the petty problems.
You just let Princess in here because her daddy has the purse
strings to Brick House. You know she's faking it!"

"What?" Princess was stunned.

"Fake, fake, fake! Fake as those boobs of hers! Plastic as
her Daddy's American Express card."

"Are you implying that Deana is not mentally ill, and I am
merely allowing her to stay because of her father's wealth and
influence?"

"Boy, you're perceptive. Did they teach you that at grad
school?"

"Reno, you are obviously harboring a lot of anger."

"And you are obviously harboring someone who does not
need to be here. I mean, I think I can speak for us all when
I say it wouldn't be so bad if she were just faking it, but the
stuff you let her get by with!"

"Such as?"

"She doesn't have to do chores. She has better leave privileges, yet we've all been here longer. She does whatever she
pleases, whenever she pleases. You never put her on the spot

like you do with us. She's faking it, and you know it!"

"Reno, I hate to burst your bubble, but you have to have a physician's referral in order to live at Saint Jude's."

"Throw enough money at a doctor and he'll tell you what you want to hear."

Just beneath where his hairline would have been if he had hair, I saw a thin layer of sweat starting to form on Big Daddy, as if he were starting to wonder if Reno were right. His mouth fell to the side like he had taken a bite of a bad piece of fish, and his eyes became evasive. His hands twitched.

"I should beat you completely senseless right now," Reno told Princess.

"You're just white trash."

"That's enough! This session isn't going anywhere. Reno, I will take your objections into consideration. In the meantime, I think that you and Deana owe each other an apology."

Silence. Neither side was going to budge.

"Very well. Take some time to think it over. You are all dismissed."

He tried to make a dignified exit, but if you looked closely, you could tell he was heading off to lick his wounds.

Group therapy was canceled for the next couple of days. Big Daddy said he wanted to be sure to give us time to cool off. I think it was because he was afraid to talk to Reno.

The decision came down on a movie night. Everyone except Princess was present. She had been sent home on leave, of course. The opening credits rolled when Big Daddy stopped the film and stood in front of the large screen television.

"I have some news," he cleared his throat. "Deana, or as you call her, Princess, won't be coming back to Saint Jude's."

All of the air was sucked out of the room.

"Come again?" Isaac asked.

"You heard right," he continued. "When I'm wrong, I admit that I'm wrong. I have given Reno's accusations consideration and found that I have been pandering to Deana's social status.

I checked her medical records. Her symptoms are vague and inconclusive and are probably not conducive to clinical depression. There are those with more serious mental illnesses that need our space. At least, that's the way I approached it with her father. He agreed with me. Now, are there any further questions?"

"You know what?" A smile crept its way onto Reno's face. "I think you're going to be all right."

Chapter 14

Males and females may not visit together in bedrooms.

Although it wasn't a Friday night, we had a special Castaways meeting. A celebration of sorts.

"Ladies and gentlemen," Reno began. "I say that the victory has been won and the island is now secure!"

"What do you think will happen to her?" Isaac asked.

"I don't care. She's gone," Reno said.

"But I mean, she wasn't all that bad."

"The hell, you say," Reno was appalled. "Yes, she was that bad. She was very, very bad. And we know you're only taking up for her because you had a crush on her."

"I mean, she was a good-looking girl," Blaine concurred, "but man, what a mouth."

"I hearby declare this a new era for Brick House," Reno said.

"Now if we can just get Big Daddy to loosen up."

"Still, I say it was classic, the way you let him have it in group therapy," Blaine said. "Brilliant."

"A girl can only take so much," Reno said.

"I don't know, though," Blaine said. "It was too easy. I'll bet he just moved Princess for her own protection. You were about to bash her head in."

"What? Just because I don't let myself get pushed around, suddenly I'm 'dangerous?' That would never happen to someone who didn't have a shrink."

Big Daddy called, annoyed, from downstairs. He was on to our meetings and admonished that this was a school night. On the way out, Blaine grabbed me by the arm and whispered that he'd see me later tonight. I didn't think he was serious until I heard a vague scratching at my door sometime around midnight.

"Can I come in?"

I sat up, but found that he was already standing in my bedroom.

"I can't sleep," he said. Was that the best excuse he could come up with? "Were you asleep?"

"No."

"Me neither. Actually, I'm kind of excited about Princess being out of here. Especially for Isaac. I mean, he was getting kind of hung up on her."

"Must be awful to have it that bad for someone."

"Yeah, must be."

He sat at the corner of my bed and propped his elbow on my knee. It was a new world for me. The craziness isolates you, and then you end up not knowing how to act.

"I enjoyed hearing you play the guitar yesterday," he said.

"When did you hear me play?"

"I just came to the top of the stairs. I was afraid that if you saw me you'd stop."

"I don't like to play in front of people."

"Why not? You're good enough."

Good enough for what? To make a fool out of myself like I did at the state fair?

"Taylor, there's an open mike night at the Expresso Café in Asheville. Why don't you play there?"

"Big Daddy will never go for it. Too many weirdos hang out there."

"They're not weirdos, they're artists."

His fingers gingerly rubbed my knee. I was glad my legs were under the covers because I hadn't shaved in weeks.

"Big Daddy is going to find you," I stammered, "and he'll assign you chores to Kingdom Come."

"I don't mind."

I twirled my hair.

"Taylor, do you realize that you are gifted?"

"I'm also crazy."

"All the famous musicians were crazy. Mozart was crazy. Beethoven—he had manic depression, just like you. You've got that same fire in you, and I'm so jealous because I want to have it in me. I don't have a gift like you do."

"I'm a far cry from Mozart."

"Taylor," he slapped his hand on the bed. "Don't you understand? You gotta find that balance. The balance that makes you functional without dampening your creativity."

"Dampening my creativity?"

"Drugs. They dampen everything. If I had talent like you, I wouldn't take my medicine half the time. All the great poets and writers composed while they were manic."

"How'd you learn so much about these famous crazy people?"

"I've been playing this game a long time, girl."

From nowhere, tears started to well. They simmered inside of me as I tried to bite them back. "But what you don't understand . . ." I started. My shoulders jerked, and I knew even though it was dark, Blaine could tell that they were quaking.

"What's the matter?"

"I. . .I. . ." Deep breath, concentrate. "What if I play and no one likes me? What if I mess up?"

"If you mess up? If they could do it, then they'd be the ones onstage. You've got to get over this. That talent of yours is too beautiful to waste."

I smiled.

"I'll let you sleep." He stepped forward and kissed me on the forehead. "You have the voice of an angel. The angel of Saint Jude."

He closed the door a little further than Big Mama would have liked.

The next morning Reno was unusually silent as we brushed our teeth in the big dorm bathroom. The mirror wasn't made of glass. It was this high polished slab of stainless steel that made your face look kind of pudgy and warped like those funhouse mirrors.

Then suddenly, uninterrupted, as she was combing her hair: "Blaine."

There was a long pause.

"What about him?"

"Don't get me wrong. I love Blaine. He's like my brother. God knows I've seen him come a long way since he came to Brick House. Know why Blaine and I get along so well?"

I shrugged.

"It's platonic. Romantically, Blaine is not what you need. You've got to watch out for these pretty boys. Any guy that spends more time in front of the mirror than you do is bad news."

Chapter 15

Saint Jude seeks to serve as a bridge between your parents, your healthcare providers and you . . .

Big Daddy called the conference during supper. It was late notice, probably so as not to allow us any time to form a protest group.

"Today we are going to take a step toward the contribution of others. Remember your therapists, your doctors? They all had to learn from someone. Today we have the opportunity to give something back to the profession. At tonight's therapy session we will have student nurses from the Smoky Ridge Community College. They are visiting Saint Jude's as a part of their study on psychiatric nursing. There will only be about five of them. They will retain strict confidentiality, as always. I'm even planning on letting them run the session."

"I don't want to talk to some stupid student," Reno cried. "That's not what we're paying for."

"I assure you that I will be on hand to help with the session and to direct it, should the need arise."

"Why do we have to do this anyway?" Blaine asked.

"These are students, and they have to learn from somewhere. You would be returning all the kindnesses shown to you by mental health professionals."

"But what if my mental health professionals have all been bastards?"

"You'll have to deal with that in therapy, Mr. Ward."

There was a brief Castaways meeting held after the announcement to discuss the implications.

For the first time, I saw Isaac twitch. It was without doubt the strangest thing I have seen in my life. It started when Big Daddy made the announcement, and Isaac shifted uncomfortably in his chair. His eyes were focused on something that only he could see. But it wasn't just in his eyes, it was in his entire body. His shoulders slouched forward. His head started to droop. He softly muttered under his breath—it was gibberish mostly, although I did pick up something about a cat.

"The thing that gets me," Blaine said, "is that these student nurses are expecting to see some sideshow freaks. Worse, Isaac is really bad off today, and he's going to give them a real performance."

"What we must do." Reno formed her words deliberately, "is give them exactly what they came to see. They want a show, we'll give them one."

"Sounds great to me," Blaine smiled.

"And you have to do it, too," Reno shook her finger at me. "In the past you've been kind of lukewarm on Castaway commitment, and I expect an Oscar-caliber production out of you."

"Don't worry."

We never have any food at group therapy sessions—Big Daddy doesn't even allow us to have sodas in there, but he made an exception and the red carpet was laid out for our student nurses. There were these little cupcake things and Greek wedding cookies along with chips and dip. Blaine made a beeline for the food, but a disapproving glance from Big Daddy made him back off.

The nurses looked younger than I ever imagined. The one that came in and sat across from me looked like she was no more than twelve. The nurses sat in the circle on the opposite side of us, opening their fresh, new Stuart Hall notebooks, reviewing questions on their little index cards.

"On behalf of the staff here, I would like to welcome you

to Saint Jude. It is a pleasure to have you here," Big Daddy said. Then he spread his arms wide, as if he were attempting to embrace them. "I hope that this will be a learning experience for all of us. We have a wide variety of symptoms here, ranging all the way from schizo affective disorder to garden variety depression."

Reno gave an annoyed clearing of her throat. "Garden variety?" she whispered.

"Mary, I believe you decided to lead us off."

"Certainly," I noticed her hand trembling as she thumbed through her cards. "How are you doing?"

The question shocked us by its absurdity. Sure, we were all doing fine. That's why we all had psychiatric records an inch thick.

"Fine," Reno responded.

"Fine," Blaine and Isaac followed suit.

"Ditto," I said.

"Have you been having any difficulties you'd like to talk about?"

I couldn't wait.

"Well, I don't see it as a difficulty, but my doctors do," I said.

"Oh, really?" Her face broadened with intrigue. "What is that?"

"My friends."

"Your friends?"

"Yeah, he doesn't like my friends."

"Describe your friends."

"Well, there's not really much to it. They're little purple bugs."

"Little purple bugs."

"Well, they kind of look like caterpillars."

"I see."

All the students were scribbling furiously in their notebooks. I stole a glance at Big Daddy. He hung his head in his hands.

"How many of them do you see?" A freckled girl in the back raised her hand.

"Sometimes only ten. Other times as much as thirty or forty. I'm not sure though. I haven't really counted."

"What do they do?"

"They come up and whisper things in my ear."

"Bad things?"

"No, no! Good things. They cheer me up when I'm down, they give me self-confidence. They do a world of good. Better than these therapy sessions."

"Is that all they do?" Mary asked.

"No, they hang with me. They go to movies with me, they party with me—they just hang with me."

"Did you ever," and Mary's lips posed hovered in a syllable, as if she were even afraid to announce this, "did you ever try to pick one of them up and squash them?"

"Why would I want to hurt my friends?"

Their focus slowly turned from me toward Blaine. I looked. During my whole tirade, he had been slowly nibbling at his wrist. He made a gurgling sound, as someone's stomach makes before they throw up.

"I see . . . Blaine?" Mary asked, "Is your name Blaine?"

Blaine responded without even bothering to take his hand out of his mouth.

"Why are you eating your hand?"

"Mrmph mmm. Tastes good," Blaine sputtered.

She didn't waste any more time on Blaine. A nurse or two raised their hand to ask questions, but she ignored them and went on to Isaac, who was sitting in his chair, legs crossed, hands in his lap, posed like he was in a job interview.

"And your name?"

He was catatonic. Unresponsive.

"It says here your name is Isaac Peterson."

"There are so many of them." His eyes scanned the room.

"So many of what?"

"Hands. Just so many hands."

Sensing that they were closing in on Isaac, Reno started with a low growl, then rose into a bark. At first it was like one of those little yappy dogs, but as the barking continued, it grew to be more like a boxer. Reno jumped from her seat almost into Mary's lap. Startled, the young woman held up her chart, as if it were some kind of shield.

Reno apparently decided that it was time for group therapy to end, because she dove to the floor and started gnawing away at Blaine's ankle. Blaine screamed and cried as if he were in immense pain.

Of course, I had to join in. Had to show my dedication to the Castaways. I pretended my friends had returned.

"My friends!" I squealed. "You're stepping on my friends!" I went around acting as if I were gathering them up into my hands, one by one.

I'm not sure how long the chaos continued until Big Daddy did something. The only thing I know was that I had turned around and he was looming over us, tall and forbidding. The nurses were gone, shuffled outside during our screaming and crying.

"Bravo," he said, clapping. "That deserves an Oscar, at least."

"What are you going to do with us?" I asked.

"Just . . . just go to your rooms." He gave a frustrated wave of his hand. "I'll figure out what to do later."

We turned single file out of the room, except Reno who was lagging behind. She turned to Big Daddy, gave a loud, annoyed, bark and then ran down the hallway.

We stayed in our rooms all evening until lights out. Not a peep from Big Daddy. Reno sneaked downstairs and told me that he was so flustered he couldn't even speak.

I was drifting into the subtle shades of sleep when I heard a gentle rap at the door. Castaways meeting, it must be. But I saw Blaine standing in the dim glow of the nightlight. He was wearing pajamas with the top unbuttoned.

"Hi, I, uh," he stopped to clear his throat like he didn't know how to begin. "Great piece of work today. I loved it."

"Thanks. I knew you'd be proud."

"I, uh, just wanted to apologize about the volleyball thing with Princess. I shouldn't have dragged you into it."

"It's all right." I said it before I even thought. No, it's not all right. He put me in Big Daddy's bad book and now I'll be stuck here for a longer time because of him. "Is something bothering you?" I asked.

"Well, yeah. You know how we were talking about how I don't want to leave here?"

"Yeah, I remember. I think you really are nuts."

"Well, before, I would never take my medication because it made me a real zombie. But the doc has offered me something else. Some new drug for schizos. It's supposed to work real well."

"So?"

"It's finally hit me. I can hold down a job again, I will be myself again."

"So why are you telling me all this?"

"I've been adjusting the doses of my medication. I've been real slick about it, so Big Daddy and Big Mama don't suspect a thing. Besides, they can't make you take your medication."

I felt sure that somehow they could make you, but I didn't say anything.

Blaine laughed, "You are so much different from anyone I've ever met. I've never met someone as talented as you are."

"You don't meet too many people."

"No, I mean," he rolled back his head and sighed, "I think you could make it. I really think you could."

"Wannabe musicians are a dime a dozen."

"You'll never know unless you try."

"I don't want to spend my life playing pop tunes at—"

"No, *your* tunes. Have you ever thought about getting them published?"

"No."

"Well, you should."

No one had ever encouraged me to explore my music. Mom looked upon it as a good diversion to keep my mind off of its self-destructive journey. But it was not practical, it was not something that I could make a living at. I was constantly encouraged and reminded that my music was "nice"—nice in the way of what you say when you get a gift you really don't like, but you don't want to hurt the feelings of the person who gave it to you. So you tell them it's just "nice."

Nice is the worst word in the English language.

"Well," he paused, "good night."

He kissed me softly on the cheek and left.

Chapter 16

We will gladly provide your family with information on support groups, since they may be suffering along with you . . .

Christmas was little more than a vague rustling of papers. Mom and I had the traditional Christmas dinner, then the relative thing, and the Santa Claus thing. Mom still leaves me stuff by the fireplace from Santa, even though she knows I'm way too old to play this game.

But what gets to me is that Mom still plays it. I'll thank her for whatever Santa has brought and she'll simply say, "It wasn't me, it was Santa." The angriest I think Mom ever got with me was when she said this and I exploded. "There is no Santa Claus, dammit!" I cried. I think it was the "dammit" that really got to her.

But this year "Santa" brought me some new music books, so I spent most of my time picking some tunes on the guitar, which was a great way to avoid conversation. I didn't get Mom anything for Christmas, since I had no money. So I wrote her a song. It was only a few chord progressions, but Mom seemed to think it was beautiful, and it touched her to tears. Call the hokey Christmas police.

After Kaye died, Mom went into therapy—though she won't admit this to anyone and tried to hide it from me—mainly because she blamed herself. She'd already bought Kaye a Christmas present for that year, and every year she pulls it out of the attic with all the other decorations and places the package by the tree, as if at any minute she will come walking through the door and unwrap it.

But after I unwrapped my present and found the music from "Santa," conversation found me, as Mom wandered into the living room with her ever-present cup of Earl Grey tea.

"Do you like it there?" She was blunt and matter-of-fact.

"Where?"

"Saint Jude, silly."

"It's okay," I wouldn't dare tell her about my blossoming romance with Blaine. To fall in love with a boy who is "crazy." It would be easier if I were in love with a black guy.

"But just okay? Not great? What kind of stuff are they filling your head with?"

"I have therapy."

"And? What are you working on there?"

"I won't tell you what I'm working on in therapy."

"Why not?"

"That's the point of therapy. If I told my mother about everything, then what's the point of having a therapist?"

"Well, I think you're doing better. You should make a try to go to school again. You're not that far behind."

"I can catch up. It's not like it's that hard or anything."

"What I'm saying is that it's very important that you make good grades."

"I always do. Not that you ever notice."

"Taylor! I notice all your grades. It's just that I miss you. I don't get to see you any more. I don't know what's going on with your life."

You don't keep me under your thumb, I felt like saying, and I almost did. But I only had one more day before I went back to Brick House, and what's the point in rocking the boat when I was so close to seeing Blaine again?

"It's just that with Kaye gone . . ."

"Mom, I'm not Kaye. Stop trying to make me into her."

I just started playing the guitar. Mother eventually left the

room when she grew tired of hearing me play.
Silent night. Yeah, right.

Chapter 17

At Saint Jude, we believe in the value and sanctity of human life . . .

When I entered Brick House, the atmosphere was different, though I couldn't exactly place my finger on what it was. Reno was her old self, talking nonstop about the ski trip she and her mother took to Cataloochee. Blaine had gotten a neat new watch—one of those fake Rolexes they sell on the streets of New York. Isaac had a good visit with his folks along with his grandparents in Georgia. But it was Big Daddy who mystified us. The way he would amble around the room without clear thought or direction, the way he would mutter silently to himself. The way he always looked as if he were focusing on some object in the distance.

When he called the group meeting immediately after we arrived, we thought we were in for it. It was finally time for him to get us back for our episode with the student nurses. Instead, he simply took a seat and folded his hands as if in prayer.

"I have some disturbing news," he began, and all of us drew our breath. One of us had been committed. That had to be what this was all about. "Deana, the young lady that you so 'affectionately' referred to as Princess, committed suicide over the holidays."

There was no air in the room. It was oppressively hot. She couldn't be dead. She was too busy worrying about the shade of her lipstick and the latest sale at the Limited to be dead.

From the corner of my eye I saw Reno turn stark white. Princess wasn't faking it.

"I don't want to go into details, but she took an overdose of her anti-depressant medication. By the time her parents came home from the Christmas party, she was already unconscious. They got her to the hospital but it was too late. There was no note. I met her parents at the hospital. Needless to say, they went all to pieces."

Then he gives this dramatic pause, as if he can't resist even using this thing to play and pawn us around. He leaned back and took a few quick breaths like you would if starting a cigarette. He had a full hand and now he was playing it, card by card, at our expense.

"I thought we could send flowers to the funeral home. I sent some and signed all your names to it," he said it flatly, as if we were also supposed to be grateful for him sending our sympathies to the family of someone we didn't even like. "I think it would be appropriate if we all went to the funeral. It will be tomorrow. And for God's sake, wear something appropriate." He cut a glance toward Reno.

Big Daddy wanted me to bring my guitar and play something at the funeral, but I said Princess didn't like my music when she was alive, and she sure wouldn't like it after she was dead. We even had a little memorial service for her at Brick House, complete with candles and some of Reno's incense.

There was time for us to say a few words about her, but most of us couldn't. We didn't want to recognize that Deana shared a common bond with us. We shared a common emotion; we felt the burning.

Isaac was the only one who had the guts to say anything. His medication had been adjusted again and it seemed to guard him against personality changes, but in the interim making him somewhat glassy-eyed and vacant.

"Deana, I mean she just, wow . . ." and he rocked on the balls of his feet. "She was a babe. I mean, a real babe." He didn't say it, but we could tell he was talking about those enormous hooters of hers. "But man, what—what a mouth that girl had. If she could just shut up and look pretty. But then she opens that mouth and, whoa!"

I expected Big Daddy to raise a cry of protest, but he said nothing, as if, coming from Brick House, it was an appropriate farewell.

After the service I went to my room to strum a few chords on my guitar,. When I entered the room I found Reno lying on my bed, staring at the ceiling.

"You know what it's like . . ." she began, ". . . know what it's like to find somebody that's only half-alive and half-dead? They kind of flounder in between for awhile, like a fish does when it's taken out of water. But after a while, they quit, like they're resigned to their fate."

"Come on, you didn't even like Princess."

"I'm not talking about Princess, I'm talking about Joan." She shifted her weight to her side and looked at me. "Under this bed you'll find bloodstains on the floor. It's from when Joan committed suicide, and I found her."

Silence. I mean, what can you say after that?

"Joan was the kind of person who grew on you. She was bipolar, just like you. That's why I'm kind of nervous about you. Afraid I'll find you lying in a pool of blood like I did Joan.

"The first thing I did was scream for Big Daddy, who called 911. The only thing I could think of was to mop up the blood, stop her from bleeding. I grabbed the corner of the bedspread and smothered her with it. She was unresponsive. Her eyes had glazed over. No one has any idea how she got a hold of the razor. It was a real job, too, not one of these little cat scratch numbers. This was a genuine slash down the length of her arms. She had placed her wrists in buckets of water so that the blood couldn't clot. The only thing I kept thinking was that it had to hurt like hell.

"She died like Princess. Died before anyone could say they were sorry or say I love you. Big Daddy is probably really and truly freaked. This isn't a very good track record for him; two Brick House alumni six feet under.

"But it's like there are some people that are broke so bad, you just can't fix them, and any attempt to just makes them all the worse. It's people like that you've got to watch out for. They'll pull you into their own private hell. Strange thing is, you don't mind going at first, so you follow them down until you realize where you are. But by then it's too late to get out."

"Reno, I'm not going to commit suicide. I'm not going to drag you down with me."

"I know you're not," she turned to leave. "You're not because I'm not going to let you."

Chapter 18

A therapist will be available to you at Saint Jude twenty-four hours a day. He will have immediate access to a hospital and a psychiatrist . . .

I wasn't all that surprised by Big Daddy's resignation three days later. You could just tell from watching him that he was merely a shadow of his former self. He often talked to himself. In our therapy sessions he would gaze absentmindedly at the doors, as if he expected someone to walk through any minute.

He had patients that committed suicide before and it didn't bother him, at least not unreasonably so. But this time, he felt as if the suicide was a direct result of his action, Big Mama told us, and if he hadn't expelled Princess from Brick House, maybe she would still be alive.

Blaine said that sometimes at night he could hear him in the kitchen, and Blaine suspected he was drowning his sorrows with wine, although he couldn't prove it because there were no bottles and, of course, alcohol was strictly forbidden at Brick House.

Big Daddy had a world that was so finite, so detailed, and for the better part of his life, he was able to keep those details alive. But when Princess died, they crumbled and left him a tattered mess.

Once, when I was the first at the breakfast table, he was sitting drinking black coffee, and he hadn't even shaved. He was wearing a plaid flannel bathrobe. His dark eyes just vaguely

107

acknowledged me, and then he returned to his room.

This brought about an important meeting of the Castaways. Big Daddy had a grip of steel that was far too manipulative to be ethical, and we were to be sure that history wouldn't repeat itself. In the meantime Brick House had contracted services with a lady from the mental health center. She was okay, but had this wide-eyed Waltons look, and you were afraid if you showed her how nasty your soul really was, she'd melt away.

"What I want to know is where they found him. I mean, what a goof," Blaine said.

"He just needed a place to stay while he was going through that divorce," Reno said.

"I don't know. I think he could've found a better place to stay than this."

"Shut up."

We tactfully decided that the newcomer, whoever he was, would have to know, simply and succinctly, that we were in charge. We'd explain to him that the rules had been changed. That we were allowed to watch R-rated movies and stay up past ten on school nights. After all, as Reno said, we outnumbered him and besides, we were all crazy. We were all like prisoners. We could riot at any minute. Big Mama, we felt, could care less about what we did as long as we left her alone.

But who knew we would get Dalton?

I had started attending school for half days at a time. Other than a few strange stares here and there, I managed quite well. Whenever I started feeling shaky, I would take a Klonopin, and it would ease the feelings, though leave me somewhat doped up in the process.

Big Mama had dropped me off at Brick House and told me that she had to go grocery shopping.

"You're leaving me alone in the house?"

"No, Dalton's there."

"Who's Dalton?"

"The new therapist."

I walked into Brick House and already I could tell things were different. The air had a thick, salty taste to it, like it does when you come in from the beach. He was so obvious I almost didn't notice him. He was sprawled on the couch in such a massive tangle of arms and legs that I couldn't see his face for his forearm stretched across his eyes.

"Excuse me, are you . . ."

A loud grumble came in return. He was wearing what would have been a right smart outfit, if he had his Oxford shirttail tucked in and his slacks not been in such a wrinkled disarray. He wore white socks, one of which had a hole in the toe, peering out at its new surroundings from his Birkenstocks.

"I'm Taylor."

He started to reply but paused. He moved his forearm and a pair of green, penetrating eyes shone through.

"You're the bipolar patient."

"Yes."

"I read your file. Hell of a file."

I had a feeling Big Daddy had been less than flattering.

"You must be Dalton—"

"Shhhhh." He drew it out long and hissy, like a snake, "I just got through driving thirteen hours straight from the coast. I got in a few hours ago and I need some rest before I take a machine gun and go up and down the street nailing people. Understand?"

I didn't know what to say. Machine gun? Nailing people? This guy was crazier than we were.

"Duck."

"What?" I asked.

"Duck," he turned and rolled on his side to face me. He had shoulder length hair that was curly in the back and his chin sported a well-trimmed sandy brown beard. I checked his left hand. He wasn't married. But then, I didn't think they'd send us a married one.

"Taylor, I have been living on a small town on the coast outside of another small town called Duck. Ever heard of it?"

"No."

"Well, I've been all around the world, mind you, and I have never tasted fried clams like this anywhere. The best. Of course, there's nothing else around except some mom and pop stores with the prices hiked so high it's ridiculous. Know how much they wanted for a pack of tampons?"

My eyebrows raised.

"Well, not for me, of course. For my girlfriend. Now run along and do your homework or watch TV—no, don't watch TV because I'm going to take a nap."

"Your bedroom's in back. Why don't you sleep there?"

"Because I don't think I have the strength to make it down the hall," he said. Then I notice his suitcases are piled in the living room.

I headed upstairs to finish some algebra so I would have free time to play my guitar. He was snoring before I made it up the staircase.

We had pizza that night even though it wasn't pizza night. A first sign that Big Daddy was long gone. Dalton kept to himself, unloading his suitcases after a lengthy afternoon nap. No one said anything to him. It was like having a foreign exchange student in your house, and you're so hesitant because you don't know about their customs or what they eat or drink, and you're so worried about offending them you just sit and stare.

He drank coffee with his pizza. Straight and black. He picked away at the mushrooms and said he didn't want to eat anything that was a fungus. He carefully avoided looking anyone in the eye.

I knew there had been a mistake. This guy was actually an escaped convict that posed as a therapist. Or a con man.

Or even worse . . .

He could actually be a psychologist.

"What's your last name?" Reno asked.

"You don't want to know," he said as he drank his coffee.

"West. Dalton West. Sounds like a bad Western movie actor." He shook his head.

"The last therapist we had," Blaine interjected, "we called Big Daddy Warbucks. Mind if we call you Big Daddy?"

"Mind if I call you jackass?"

There was a strained silence. Big Daddy rarely cussed.

"We freak you out, don't we?" Reno was geared up to play a mind game with him.

"Let me tell you something," he started. "I had a patient who took a chainsaw and cut off his leg. To the waist."

Even Reno fell silent.

"Anyway," Dalton talked with his mouth full, "this same guy could cook an awesome bunch of fried clams."

"I certainly hope you won't go around telling others what I'm doing at Brick House."

"Reno," he gave a crooked half smile, "don't flatter yourself. No one wants to hear your story that bad. Except me, of course, and that's mainly because they're paying me."

That's all the material we needed for our minds to think up stories about him that would fill a thousand Castaway meetings. He was on suspension because he'd done it with a patient and the church board just didn't know about it. He was kicked out of Duck for dealing drugs illegally to patients. He had no degree and faked everything on his resumé.

He cleared his place and headed back toward his room.

"Where are you going?" Blaine asked.

"I'm going to finish unpacking."

"But we have group time after supper."

"I thought therapy sessions were in the afternoons."

"They are. You skipped today's."

"Oops. Hope no one had a crisis." Dalton was unfazed.

"These group times are daily temperature readings to see how we function as a community," said Blaine. We snicker because we know he's imitating Big Daddy. "Here at Saint Jude we view ourselves as a family, and this is our chance to work out our problems and frustrations with each other before we get out of control."

Dalton paused for a minute. His eyes rolled toward the ceiling as if he were doing some deep thinking.

"Right," he said. "Everyone gather in the living room."

We gathered in our usual space, and we found that he preferred the couch to Big Daddy's recliner. That meant two of us, Reno and I, had to share the recliner while he sprawled over the couch.

"Okay, group time. Everybody know each other's name?"

"Yes." Our replay was distant and whitewashed.

"Does anybody have a major crisis?"

"I failed an algebra quiz," Isaac said.

"Crisis, man, I said crisis. You haven't set your hair on fire or anything like that?"

"No."

"Then don't complain."

"I don't like your attitude," Reno said.

"Why? Because I won't coddle you like Richie Rich or Big Warbucks or whatever the hell you called him? I've got news for you. In the real world, people could care less if you're mentally ill. The only thing they care about is how are you able to function, how you are able to work, to produce, to get good grades, pay the bills. No exceptions. That means you fail tests, get evicted, the power gets cut off, and you've got a bad credit rating with Southern Bell. I'm not teaching you how to sugar coat your sickness. I'm teaching you how to survive. Anyone who tells you something different is selling you something."

Silence.

"Now, finally, is anybody ticked off at anybody else?"

There was a long pause before our hoarse reply, "No."

"Okay, group time is over. I'm going to get another cup of coffee and something to eat."

He leaped from the couch with amazing agility and went to the kitchen, leaving us alone to cradle our silent room.

Chapter 19

The professional services of a therapist will be available at group therapy . . .

Group therapy with Dalton was like watching a baseball no-hitter. We could bring our problems and complaints to him, and he would make us see that there really was a simple explanation for everything and our world really wasn't falling apart at the seams. It was kind of frustrating because you spend your nights crying over something, gradually building up a bonfire. Then Dalton spits in it and puts out the blaze.

Watching Dalton was like watching a professional Shakespearean actor—every move was well orchestrated. The lines were timed impeccably.

He also drank more coffee than anyone I've ever known.

We think it was Dalton who finally convinced Blaine to take more responsibility for his life.

"You are such a wimp!" he said, causing Blaine's head to bob in surprise. "You have been stabilized on medication for a long time. You just pull these stunts so you won't have to face the real world. I got news for you, if you think you're going to get married and live here at Saint Jude, you got another think coming."

Dalton smoked, too, although it wasn't allowed. He didn't seem to care. It really made Big Mama angry because she ended up cleaning his ashtrays that he had scattered around the house, and she had to mask the smell of smoke from the entrance hall.

I went on a brief tirade about how the guys in school hated me and I was always the social outcast; too awkward to belong, too naive to be in the know. Not even God cared.

"Taylor, I'll make a deal with you. Why don't you let God go to high school, and you can run the universe? Or better yet, let me go to your high school and you can deal with all these nutty people."

We suppressed gasps. We knew it was definitely not kosher for a therapist to call us nutty. But coming from Dalton, it was a strange kind of compliment. As if the whole world were insane, and we were the only ones good enough to admit it.

"But what do I do when they make fun of me?" I asked.

"Educate them. Let them know the truth of the matter instead of their stupid little rumors. The truth is light. It floods the corners of the soul, which leaves little room for darkness. Most people, if educated, will make the right decisions—if they know the truth."

"But what if I try that and it still doesn't work?"

"Then tell them to kiss your ass."

"But I can't do that," I responded.

"Then have them call me," Dalton gave me a wink, "and I'll tell them to kiss mine. That's it. Therapy's over."

He exited the room with a cup of coffee in one hand and a cigarette in the other.

Chapter 20

We have a variety of social activities planned for you at Saint Jude that should prove entertaining and build your self-esteem.

It went without saying that you never got invited to New Year's Eve parties if you were at Brick House. No one wanted to have you around unless it was for comic relief.

Dalton made a motion that we throw our own New Year's Eve party at Brick House, but for some reason, the hats and party favors weren't enough to make it a real holiday. Dalton said fine, have it our way, spend the evening with Dick Clark, that miserable S.O.B. (Dalton never really elaborated on why he hated Dick Clark so much.) Big Mama left early for the evening, and Dalton whisked some groceries into his room that Blaine and I suspected were to be used to create some whiskey sours. Reno somehow managed to get an unsupervised date with her man (as long as she was home by midnight) and Isaac had crashed early due to a stomach virus.

Blaine and I went out on the fire escape—the night was unusually mild—and glanced at the stars. Blaine said he wanted to take an astronomy class at the university, and he started talking about Einstein and theories about space and time—stuff that was way over my head. I just plunked a few chords on my guitar.

"Brick House doesn't have holidays," he said. "No matter how many parties they offer you at church, no matter how many people you've invited, they never seem to be the same. It's like a jigsaw puzzle you work so hard to complete and then realize that you're missing the final piece."

"Dalton's gonna be three sheets gone tonight," I said. "Let's do something really childish like put his boxers in the freezer."

"How do you know he wears boxers?"

"You can just tell. He's a boxer guy."

"How can you tell?"

"The scraggly hair, the personality, the whole thing, it just screams boxers."

"Do you think he's smoking weed tonight?"

"Surely he's not that stupid."

"He's smart; he knows he's the captain on a sinking ship."

"What do you mean?"

"Taylor, don't tell me you haven't picked up on it."

"On what?"

"Saint Jude. It's going to hell in a handbasket."

"Huh?"

"Princess is dead. Joan's dead. Isaac is getting worse. Plus, have you noticed that no one's come in to replace Princess? This place is supposed to have a waiting list, and that empty bed's been sitting there."

"Blaine, do you really think. . .?"

"Something's up. I'll bet they're going down the tubes."

"Why?"

"Come on, this is a dumping ground for upper middle class black sheep. Can't send us to a group home in Asheville. No, that would be too scary. They'd feel too guilty putting us in there with God knows what. But Saint Jude, now that's different. It's expensive, it's like a resort, and it's not really a group home, which avoids awkward dinner party conversation when you're asked 'what is Blaine up to?'"

"I think Mom dumped me a long time ago."

"Taylor, what's the absolutely worst thing that has ever happened to you?"

I strummed my silver melody, hoping he wouldn't notice that I was still trying to digest the question.

"Well?"

"It was when my sister died."

"She was in a car accident, wasn't she?"

"Yeah. Tractor trailer jackknifed and it caught her. It was on I-40 like you're going to the Pigeon River Gorge. It congested up traffic so bad that the ambulances had a hard time getting through. She died instantly. Mom was in ICU for a week. You'd think that after that, Dad would realize what he had almost lost, and be thankful for what he still had, but instead, he just blamed it on her. She should've done this, she should've done that. It made me realize what a jerk he could be. That was when the string that brought them together broke. It was beyond fixing. Kaye was the one that kept them together, never me. I was always jealous because she kept them together for so long, and all I could do was watch their marriage disintegrate."

"You were jealous of your sister?"

"Who wouldn't be? I was the whole reason my parents got married. Mom and Dad weren't married when I was conceived. Back then, single parenthood wasn't exactly socially acceptable. They had a shotgun wedding. But when Kaye came along, they were ready to have children, and she was legit. It didn't help matters that she was beautiful and looked like a China doll."

"But that's the thing about China dolls—they break easily."

"What about you, Blaine? What's the worst thing that every happened to you?"

"It's this illness," he said, "this damn illness. It gets inside my skin and itches till there's no way I can get to it."

"What is the worst part about it?"

"Now it's not so bad, because the medicine has helped a lot, but when I was hallucinating—man, horrible sights. Like walking into a room and finding it full of broken bodies—not bloody—just broken, like dime store mannequins taken apart by a Dr. Frankenstein. I would see things move—I saw the draperies walk across the room and hang themselves. I heard voices, voices that told me to run with the devil, voices that told me I was Christ, voices that told me anything but the truth."

"And the medicine has stopped the voices."

"It stopped the voices on the inside, the voices in my head, but now I have to deal with another form of voices—the lines people keep feeding me. That I'm not going to be able to work, that I should just declare disability and forget about it. Voices that tell me I'm finished. Then there are the syrupy Peter Pan voices that tell me all is right with the world and I don't have a problem at all; voices of complete denial. Remember, Taylor, no matter what medicine you're on, there will always be the voices."

"Well, what's the *best* thing that's ever happened to you?"

"Hands down it was when my nephew was born," he said. "I never got along with my sister, but my nephew came at a time when there was a lot of conflict within my family. We were fighting over stupid stuff—spending too much time on the phone, leaving the toilet seat up—and my schizophrenia was somewhat under control with the medication.

"They wouldn't even let me hold him. You see, about the time he was born was about the same time that news story came out about the schizophrenic in Iowa that went down the street with an automatic pistol mowing down everyone in sight. They were afraid that I'd snap like that, too, even though the doctor told them I was much more likely to hurt myself than to hurt others. I'd never want to hurt anyone."

With that he gently took my hand off the strings and rubbed it against his cheek. He was working on a goatee and the hairs were sharp and sparse.

"I know you'd never hurt anyone." It seemed the thing I should say at such a moment.

"I remember holding him at the hospital after he was born. My mom and dad flanked me and my brother-in-law stood right in front of me with his hands on mine. As if I were going to suddenly start choking the little thing."

His face was closer to mine now, and I could feel the warmth of his breath upon my cheek.

"What about you, Taylor? What's the best thing that ever happened to you?"

"I learned to play the guitar. It's my hiding place, you see."

"You have a very talented hiding place. Have you thought any more about what I said? About the lithium, I mean."

"I was thinking about cutting down on my doses." Actually, I had almost forgotten about the suggestion, but I didn't want him to think that I wasn't taking him seriously.

"You were meant to soar, Taylor. You were meant to dream. You can't soar when you're being doped up."

In Blaine's eyes, all of the bad things vanished. All of the late nights crying, all of the cutting on myself, even Big Mama looking through my suitcase for sharps. In Blaine's eyes were only the good things. He and I alone together. The brilliance of my madness, that I would dot the sky like the hundreds of stars we didn't even dare to count. With Blaine I forgot all the bad things of being bipolar and thought only good thoughts.

"You can dream in music too loud for words," he said in my ear, his fingers hotly dancing on my cheek. "You are the most beautiful, burning creature I have ever seen."

His lips found their way to the base of my ear and lingered there, filling my neck with the steaming sensation of a long, hot bath. There were questions, but nothing that couldn't wait.

He pulled me toward his waist and kissed me long and full. I held tightly to my guitar, feeling that it was the only thing anchoring me to the earth and if I released it I would go sailing off into space and hit the moon.

His caresses were soft and delicate, as if he were afraid he would bruise me. They danced along my body like a well-choreographed ballet, filled with grace and artistic expression, a song in every step.

"I wish this were the most beautiful place in the world," he said. "If we were somewhere else, I'd ask you to marry me. But not here, not now. It wouldn't be right to ask you in a place like this."

Marriage? My mouth would have dropped if it weren't engaged in his lips. Of all the places to find my soulmate . . . Saint Jude.

Blaine slowly pulled away from me, and I could feel a part of myself coming loose with him. He had divided me. Now he would carry a part of me with him for always.

He glanced at his watch.

"Twelve fifteen," he grinned. "We missed it. New Year's Eve and we missed it."

He made it sound like something bad.

Chapter 21

We will deem when it will be psychologically healthy for you to leave Saint Jude's . . .

I was the first to admit that I didn't even know it was a wedding band. For starters, she was wearing it on the wrong hand. But Reno said she did that so the therapist and Big Mama wouldn't get wise. Then she finally broke down and confessed that it was actually more like an engagement ring.

"It's one of those Irish wedding bands," she said, indicating the two hands holding a heart and the crown. "It stands for loyalty, friendship and love. Or something like that. I don't quite remember. He got it at Wick and Greene, you know, the first-class jewelry shop in downtown Asheville."

"Why didn't you let us know you were getting married?"

"It's not that kind of married," she said, as if that were all the explanation necessary. "We're going to this little chapel in Gatlinburg for the ceremony and honeymoon—of course, we've already celebrated the honeymoon . . ."

"So you're leaving?" Shock and dismay battled it out for the expression on my face. If Reno left, who would take care of me?

"You'll be fine, kid," she said. "Just play the game."

The rules about when you could leave Saint Jude were very hazy. Some said you could leave as soon as you turned sixteen. Others said you had to stay until it was clear that you had yourself a job or some means of support. I also heard that you could leave as soon as you got your GED.

122

But whatever the criteria, Reno's wedding seemed to fit the description. Dalton never said a word about it—he didn't even raise a cry of protest. I almost thought he was glad to get rid of her.

"And when I get back from Gatlinburg . . ." Reno's eyes opened into saucers and she started bouncing on her bed. "He's got this house all set up in Biltmore Forest—Biltmore Forest! I mean, it is sooo posh."

"I guess it helps to marry into a wealthy family," I said.

"Hey, you can marry them rich or you can marry them poor, so you might as well marry them rich."

"But . . . do you love him?" I thought their romance was little more than a good roll in the hay.

"It's not so much love . . . it's that he completes me. When I'm upset, when the depression strikes, it's not the Prozac or the group therapy that keeps me going. It's him."

I wanted to find a way to argue with that, to say that he didn't brush his teeth enough or that he had greasy hair, but I didn't know him well enough to mount a convincing argument, and why make waves when they're not going to do you any good?

Dalton was my last chance.

"How can you let her ruin her life?" I asked. "She's got to finish school and have a career and—"

"Whoa, whoa, wait a minute, since when were you put in charge of Reno's life?"

"She's my friend, and I just want what's best for her."

"Taylor, you'll learn that sometimes in life we have to let people do what they want to do and just hope that it's what's best for them. Sometimes it works out, sometimes it doesn't."

"But he is so much older than she is."

"He's only twenty-one—what, you don't like him?"

"I like him, I guess," I said. Frankly, the only time I had seen him or spoken to hm was during their make-out session in Reno's room.

"If it makes you feel any better, I believe that Reno intends to finish school," he said. "She was talking to me about a possible career in pharmacy."

"Do you really believe that?" Hope cracked my voice.

"Taylor, sometimes we have to pretend that we believe it."

Chapter 22

Saint Jude is like a family, and when one of you leaves, it is felt by the whole group . . .

My opinion of Dalton quickly deteriorated after Reno left. Blaine kept reminding me during our late-night conversations that I should remember Big Daddy; at least Dalton didn't act like he had *Psychology Today* crammed up his butt.

I knew that many women would consider Dalton handsome, but there was something about his features that started to disgust me. His hair was never styled and you could see the split ends on his pony tail. He drank too much coffee. I was getting cancer from his secondhand cigarette smoke.

"Well, just remember that he lets us do what we want. He lets us watch R-rated movies and doesn't make us act like such perfect prissies all the time," Blaine said one night.

Dalton said there was no point in trying to shield us from R-rated movies. He said the real world was much scarier.

Isaac began slowly falling apart. His medication made him glassy-eyed, and he complained of chronic diarrhea. But when he was off his medicine, it was as if he operated on a different plane from the rest of the world. He hoarded things, sometimes pieces of string, or those little twist-ties used to close up garbage bags. You could tell him something, then two minutes later he wouldn't be aware of having talked to you. If that's what it means to get better, I'd much rather be sick.

*   *   *   *

"Dalton is going to drive this place into the ground," I said. "Reno is going to end up just like Princess. She's going to kill herself the first time a crisis comes up."

"Reno was in better shape than you are," countered Blaine. "Besides, it's not right for you to want to hold her back. I know that y'all were friends and you miss her, but Taylor, just be happy for her."

But how could you be happy for someone when you were afraid you'd never never see her again? Of course, Reno had told us that she'd come by and visit, but she said it flatly, without conviction. Like she was obligated to say it.

I don't blame her. When I leave here, I don't want to see this place again either.

I did little annoying things here and there to get back at him—nothing he could pin down on me, mind you, but like when he'd leave his cigarette burning in the ashtray and then go to get some more coffee, I would put out the cigarette. For a brief while he looked at it like he couldn't remember if he put it out or not. Sometimes I'd switch the coffee to an old can of decaf that looked like it had been on the shelf since 1980. Big Mama helped me. She didn't like Dalton either, probably because he wasn't afraid to tell her to do something, unlike Big Daddy. Dalton would often mutter that she "missed a spot" or "are you going to vacuum today?" or "just what was in this casserole anyway?" She suspected he did way too much LSD in the Sixties.

But Blaine reminded me that the reason I didn't want to give Dalton a chance was the same reason people didn't want to give me a chance. They were too quick to judge by outward appearances. He tried to get me to look at Dalton with more tolerance for what he was trying to do for St. Jude and for us, but I remained skeptical. Maybe I resented the no-nonsense way he forced me to confront unpleasant things about myself.

But all that changed the night Isaac left.

I was awakened by shouting from downstairs. At first I paid

it no mind, thinking it was Mom and Dad going at it again, but the words became richer and harbored the muffled sound of crying.

I went to the stairs and stood just out of view of a panic-stricken Isaac wandering around the room like a caged tiger, occasionally upsetting the coffee table, lamps and whatever else got into his path.

"I just can't believe they did it!" he cried. "They knew how much I hated it there!"

"Isaac, try to calm down. There's nothing you can do about it now." It was Dalton's voice, though I couldn't see him.

"I just can't believe it . . ." and he was sobbing now, in deep, erratic bursts.

"You know that's not the way I would have had it, Isaac. But your mother said she just couldn't afford this place anymore."

"Have you ever been there? Have you ever been in a state hospital?"

"I worked in one for nine years."

"Dinner is the only time men and women are together, you see, and they march you in like a police line-up. You're not allowed to talk to any girls, or even to look at them. Then beside you is this guy who's so medicated he drools all over you. You walk around like cattle. It's like you're just a number."

"If there was a way—"

"There's got to be a way! Why does this place have to be so damn expensive? I can't help it if our insurance sucks."

"I don't want to even mention this because I'm afraid it won't come through. I've talked to the board chairman about your situation. He's seeing if the church can help foot the bill for your stay here."

"Yes, then I can stay."

"Financially Saint Jude is hanging by a thread since Mr. Hays withdrew his support. They probably won't go for it. But I'll push it. I'll push it for as long as I have to."

"But tonight, why do I have to leave tonight?" Here the sobs became deeper.

"I thought it would be better to avoid a long drawn-out scene in front of the others—"

"At least here I was a part of something, a family."

"You'll find another family."

"Where? There's no place for us. Don't you understand? It's a big world but it has no place for people like us, so they just sweep us under the carpet." He was on his knees.

Dalton, his eyes red and swollen with exhaustion, walked over to Isaac and slowly helped him to his feet.

"What do you want me to tell you, Isaac? Do you want me to tell you that the world really isn't such a bad place and that everything's going to be all right? I'm not going to lie to you. The world is a terrible place. You might not get well, but you have value. Just by being human you have value, and all the rest of it, the strange quirks and the heavy medication, is just window dressing. Don't lose sight of who you are. You are not a disorder. You are a human being."

"Please, please get me back to Saint Jude . . ."

"I'll try," he said, rubbing Isaac's shoulder.

Then Isaac completely fell apart. His legs buckled and he slouched to the ground, as if he had lost all control of his muscles. Dalton caught him and cushioned his fall to the floor. I never knew a guy could cry like that. I had never seen a guy cry. Dad had cried when Kaye died, but I never saw him, just heard sobs through the bedroom door.

Then Dalton started running his fingers through Isaac's hair and humming something. It was faint and soft and I couldn't make it out. I don't have any idea how long they stayed like that, with Isaac crying on Dalton's shoulder and Dalton acting the part of the comforting mother. Eventually, Isaac's sobs became fewer and far between.

I was awake all night wondering if something like that could happen to me, and if it did, who would be there to hold me?

Chapter 23

Visits from family members are always welcome, though we do ask that you notify us in advance . . .

My father came today.

He knocked at the door, which immediately took me by surprise because there were never any visitors at Saint Jude. Dalton and I were watching the Carolina - Georgia Tech game—Dalton had a passion for the ACC. At first Dalton and I exchanged glances because we weren't sure who should answer the door. Big Mama had gone to the supermarket.

"I'll get it," he said, and he slouched forward, tucking in his shirttail as he walked across the living room in bare feet.

The familiar voice eeked out a tune, as if he were afraid of being discovered.

"I'm here to see Taylor."

Dalton brought him into the room, but kept a skeptical eye on me, as if he weren't really sure I could handle it. I nodded curtly toward my father.

"Hi," his voice was thin and hollow.

"Hi."

"I'll be in the back office if you need me." Dalton turned off the television set.

"How is she, I mean, is she doing all right?" I couldn't believe Dad had the gall to actually ask Dalton in front of me.

"All medical records are confidential. I can't discuss them without Taylor's release." I didn't know if this was true or not. I felt for sure my parents could get some information on me, but Dalton was protecting me, just like he tried to protect Isaac.

'Do you remember me, Taylor?" he asked. The question was so stupid it floored me."

"Relax, I'm not stupid, just crazy."

"You never were stupid, Taylor. You were smarter than all of us. That's why we were at a loss and didn't know what to do with you."

"What brings you here?"

"Yeah, kind of surprised to see your old man after he ran out on you."

"Mom said you're doing well with a recycling company."

"Vice-President."

"Congratulations."

"Thanks. It doesn't take much, actually. Just someone who knows the nuts and bolts of things."

"How's California?"

"It's okay. You'd like it, lots of artsy people around."

"See any celebrities?"

"I don't live in that part of California. I miss the Appalachians."

"I never knew you to be so sentimental."

"Well, I can't blame you for being mad. I deserve it. It's just that, I couldn't deal with stuff when Kaye died."

"You didn't have to blame Mom for it. It wasn't her fault."

"I know. But it was easier for me to blame her than myself. All I thought about were the things I didn't do with her. The things I didn't teach her. She was only nine. I never taught her how to dream. I never taught her that she could do anything she wanted to."

"Strange. You never bothered to teach me any of that."

"I didn't have to, Taylor. See? That's what I came here to tell you. You were different. You had a fire burning within you that no one could touch. You were restlessly creative."

"But everything with you was Kaye. She was the baby of the family."

"No, it's because she needed special attention."

"What about the help and attention I needed?"

"You were tough. We knew you were strong."

"You're just making up excuses for why you don't love me as much as you loved her."

"That's not true."

"Why are you here? Getting a guilt trip?"

He sat down across from me and folded his hands in his lap.

"I quit my job. Built up a real nice nest egg for myself. Going down to the Caribbean. Early retirement, you could say."

"Going with someone half your age, I'll bet."

"As a matter of fact, she's three months older than I am."

"Glad you weren't lonely," I tried to sound as sarcastic as possible.

"I came here to bring you something."

"I don't want anything from you."

"I know this place is expensive."

"It's a country club for those who aren't playing with a full deck. Sorry you can't stay or I'd show you the pool and tennis courts."

"I didn't expect you to be happy with me. There's no excuse for the way I treated you. I'd apologize but I know you wouldn't accept it, and you shouldn't. After all these years of neglect, it's just words."

"If you had even just put up a good act." I could feel hot tears in my eye, but I bit my lip and was determined not to cry. "If you could've just acted like you cared, or even acted like you loved me."

"I know, I know. Everything you say is true."

"I don't want your gifts."

"Hear me out, please. When I left for California, I put some investments in stocks, mutual funds. It's brought a good payoff. Thus, I'm retiring early. But I've always known you belonged in college. You're too smart to slip through the cracks,

illness or no illness. I've got an account I want you to use for
your college. I came into town to get things set up."

"I don't want your money."

"I know that money can't fix the problems I've caused, but
you've got to get an education, and your mother can't afford
it with all the medical bills."

"I can play my guitar."

"Taylor, you are talented, I know, but the guitar can't buy
you a living. You've got to do something else."

It was then that it just occurred to me that I didn't have
a calling. Blaine could talk about the stars with unbridled en-
thusiasm. Reno had a husband to make her happy. And even
Princess had her passion for the latest fashion from New York.
I had no calling. Nothing other than my guitar, which for a
job put me at about a dime-a-dozen at that.

My illness had taken my friends from me, my chance at
a normal life . . . and now it had stripped me of a calling.
Sure, there had to be a contribution I could make to the world.
But this was too much to worry about on top of my bipolar
disorder. One thing at a time.

"Taylor, have you considered what you might want to do?"

"I haven't given it a lot of thought. I've had a lot on my
mind . . . mainly being out of it."

"Promise me you'll at least think about it."

I started to say something but my hand was shaking.

"I'm upsetting you. I'd better go. I gave your mother all
the account information. It's all yours. Only you can access it.
Use it any way you want."

I didn't look at him as he turned to leave. I heard his footsteps as they scuffed over the carpet. I heard the creak of the
doorknob as he opened the door.

Then I rushed into the doorway and threw my arms around
his shoulders—even if he was too late. Maybe I shouldn't have
forgiven him so easily . . . but he was my father.

Chapter 24

We encourage your academic achievements . . .

I had everything planned for Blaine's graduation.

So what if it was January and graduation wasn't until May? I had orchestrated the whole thing in my mind. It was there that I was going to publicly declare my love for him.

I'm taking less of the medication now. Big Mama doesn't suspect a thing because I've never had a problem with medication compliance. I get a little down at times, but no worse than when I had PMS. And at times the lift can be so joyous that it makes me forget I'm a human being. It's like I'm a piece of a star that glided by the earth in a century too early to count, too early to remember.

The guys at school were starting to take notice, now that I was coming back for half days. So what if they still called me "psychobitch?" I laughed at them. They were so little in comparison to my glory. A few of them were awestruck by me. You can't make fun of someone who refuses to be offended.

I even got asked out on a date but refused because Patricia told me a rumor was going around that I had lost my virginity at Brick House and I was "easy." I strung them along like a line of beggars, laughing at the lust in their eyes. Didn't they see that sex may have been brilliant, but not as brilliant as what I was experiencing? Not that I had ever experienced sex, but I know that nothing could compare with what I was feeling.

It was as if I had lived my life as Clark Kent, and slowly, but slowly, I was becoming Superman.

My orchestration for Blaine would be nothing more than a kiss on the cheek, maybe the lips if I was feeling daring. Slip him the tongue if I'm feeling sexy. But anyway, it's the symbolism that would ring true.

He would have already finished walking across the stage, and the Brick House crew would come up to greet him. We would be there because, of course, Blaine wasn't embarrassed by us. Like he said, if they have a problem with the fact that he's a schizophrenic, screw them. Blaine had resumed compliance with his medication and was doing exceptionally well. I'd stride up right in front of the others, throw my arms around him. He'd respond, thinking this was an innocent hug, but as he brought his face down to mine I would kiss him, boldly and proudly on the lips. Lips, lips, lips, lips. They'd be soft and warm, but even sweeter than they are at night because it would be during the day, when I proclaim my love before God.

I'd surprise the other members of Brick House, by the romance that had blossomed beneath their watchful eyes.

The other women standing near Blaine would look at me and their eyes would steam over with the worst kind of jealousy. With patchwork honesty, they'd reveal that I was the one for Blaine, and Blaine the one for me. That we were more than they were. We were a couple. We were holy.

We would separate for a while, to cool their jealous hearts, and we would not come together until our secret meeting that night. That's when I'd give him his graduation present. It's a song. I wrote it especially for him. It's called "The Angel of Saint Jude" and to be honest, it's inspired by Reno's boyfriend and his ability to sneak into Brick House late at night without anyone noticing.

It's a song of many things. About how you wander down life's road, and you think you know exactly where you want to go, but life happens to you and you get lost somewhere along the way.

The excitement built up in me until I thought I'd burst. It

was like waiting for your birthday to open presents. The picture of Blaine in his black mortarboard and tassel, in his robe, looking like one of those sexy college professors. He had started growing a goatee, and by May it would probably be at least visible to the naked eye.

I couldn't wait. I hinted that I had written a song about him.

"What is it?" he joked. "'The Ballad of the Brick House Stud'?"

"No," I laughed, and then explained to him that it's about this angel, see, and he's been assigned to take care of people on earth, but he becomes too involved in the things of Earth and he becomes human, and God won't take him into heaven until he changes the life of at least one person.

In case you haven't guessed it, the person is me, Blaine is the angel, and God is our matchmaker. Nothing could make me happier.

He begged to hear it, and I said not until his graduation night. (I might plan to give him something else that night, but it depends on how he plays his cards.)

Imagine my surprise when he told me he already graduated.

It was some program through the university in Asheville, where he would be able to take his GED test and get started in spring semester classes. Of course, he aced the GED; they say schizophrenics are usually very smart.

But it was a part of his life that went on without me.

"I—I won't be around as late," he said, hesitantly. "I will have to study and stuff."

"What do you mean?"

"I mean, I may not be around at night as much as I have been." He sounded so sweet and earnest, the typical hometown boy trying to make good. But I knew it was an excuse, an excuse for a reason not to see me. A way to get out of my life. Erased.

Slowly I noticed things that seemed to disappear from his

room. First his books, then some clothes. I approached him while he was studying.

"You've been busy," I said.

"I know. I wish I was a literary type like you. It would make things so much easier."

"No, I mean your stuff. Half the closet's gone. You hardly ever stay here."

"I've got a night lab on Monday, Wednesday, and Friday. It's easier if I stay with a friend on campus."

Male or female friend he didn't specify, and I didn't have the guts to ask.

"And Dalton is okay with that?"

"Dalton's letting me out of Saint Jude," he said. "He's very pleased with my progress. My medication is working fine. As long as I keep seeing a shrink regularly, there shouldn't be any problems."

One Friday I sneaked into his room before therapy and all of his things were gone. When I asked Dalton, he said that a space had come available in an apartment. The rent was cheap, and Blaine could walk to campus.

"And you let him leave?" My eyes reflected with disbelief. The angel has left? The angel has gone on to better things? Who will take care of us? Who will watch over us?

"It's hard to let go," he said, as if he could sense the emotion that ran through my mind. "If we love him, we should be happy for him. It's been a rough life . . . he said he would visit often," Dalton tossed me a bone.

I slept that night uneasily. Blaine had never even heard the song I had written for him, but somehow, it seemed inappropriate to track him down and sing it now. So I hummed myself to sleep with it, as if there were someone there to hear.

Chapter 25

What's worst is often best, and best is often worst. You can chase yourself, as long as you don't catch yourself . . .

I played "The Angel of Saint Jude's" seven times in my room that Saturday afternoon, because when I played it I felt that Blaine was there, watching, wondering. It was better than a photograph, because what I had was an illustration of his soul. It danced in my mind like purple clouds.

I didn't sleep last night. I had had four hours sleep in the past three days. I didn't mind. I would sit up and play softly, so Dalton couldn't hear. I replayed the movie in my mind of Blaine's inevitable visit to Brick House, and how he'd take me into his arms and let me wear his oversized sweatshirt with fraternity letters on it. Then he'd tell me about classes and drinking games and panty raids.

"Bravo."

The voice was calm and flat and not entertaining. I would've dismissed it, but I heard clapping too, just from outside my window. I found Dalton outside, sitting on the fire escape where Blaine and I had made out earlier.

"How long you been playing?" he raised one eyebrow.

"A couple of years. " I was embarrassed and wondered how long he had been listening.

"Come outside. Sit a spell. It's a little nippy, but it'll be good for you. Clear out the lungs," he said as he puffed away on a cigarette.

I staggered my way outside, and found that I had to sit

uncomfortably close to Dalton, and the rumors started circulating in my mind that maybe he had left Duck because he had an affair with one of his patients.

"You really miss Blaine, don't you?" he said.

"I guess so. A little."

"A little? With him sneaking up here and you making out every night? You miss him a lot."

He knew. My cheeks burned.

"I can explain. It was really just a—"

"Taylor, I'm not your mother. You don't need to explain anything to me. I'm not here to judge. It's just that sometimes it's not a good idea for people with mental disorders to hook up, that's all."

"Why not? They can help and support each other—"

"They can destroy each other and believe me, Taylor, I have seen it happen more times than I care even to recall."

I strummed a few chords. The guitar was a great weapon when I couldn't come up with a good comeback.

"I know how you feel. I miss my girlfriend." He said it as an afterthought.

"You have a girlfriend?"

"Been dating for five years. We're engaged."

"Does she live in Asheville?"

"No, she's in a hospital," he said. " Duke University."

"I'm sorry. Does she have cancer or something?" Duke is where everyone went when they had cancer.

"No, she's got obsessive-compulsive disorder. She used to wash her hands until they were red and bleeding. She counted everything. She stopped eating because all the food was contaminated. It's a hell of a life," he sighed.

"And you're engaged?"

"Yeah. Of course, I don't know when the wedding will be. Don't even know if they'll let her out of Duke."

"Then why are you engaged?"

"It's a curse to be a man of science, Taylor. When I first

met her, she wasn't too bad off. But it gradually got worse. I was fascinated by her. I wanted to play Good Samaritan. Had to help her. I could bring peace to her mind."

"What happened?"

"Relationships are complicated things. You try to do what you think is right, but sometimes you only end up hurting the other per-son."

He blew some smoke in my face. I don't think he meant to do it on purpose. I just think he wasn't paying attention to what he was doing.

"So if she's at Duke, why are you here?"

"What can I do? I go to visit and I hold her and then she starts clawing at me, saying that I'm dirty and she needs to take a shower. When I try to prevent her from it, she starts flipping out, and pretty soon the doctor has to come with a dose of Thorazine. Puts her in La-La Land. She's so doped up after that, all we can do is just sit on the couch. I hold her and she mutters to herself. Counting over and over . . . four, five, six, pick up sticks, seven, eight, nine, stitch in time."

"Was she like this when you first met her?"

"Not really. I think I made her worse, inadvertently. Before, she was obsessive about stuff, but stuff that made sense. Did she cut off the stove? Did she cut off the lights? Did she lock the door? But gradually, it broke down."

"I'm sure it wasn't your fault."

He nodded his head as if to say "nice try."

"Taylor, you've just gotten things straightened up upstairs," he put his index finger to my temple. "You don't need some guy to come upstairs and start messing things up. Just enjoy being who you are."

"Yeah, a sideshow freak."

"There are some advantages to being a sideshow freak."

"Like what?"

"For starters, no one expects you to make any sense. That gives you the freedom to be creative. It's like for the rest of us, the world is a black and white TV set; for you, it's a Disney cartoon."

"I'll remember that." My fingers returned to the guitar.

"Have you been feeling okay, Taylor?"

"I feel better than I ever have in my life."

"You haven't been sleeping well. I hear you at night playing that guitar all the time."

"I can't sleep. Thinking of Blaine." Dalton could not find out that I was skipping lithium. Not when I was on the verge of writing my greatest song ever. "I write a lot of songs when I'm thinking of someone."

"Your talking has picked up some speed."

"What?"

"You're talking a little fast."

"No, I'm not."

"Your sentences are like a New York taxi driver."

"And what's that supposed to mean?"

"When is the next time you have your blood checked?"

My lithium level was checked every three months. I was due for another checkup in about two weeks.

"About another two months," I said.

"Two months?" he looked at me skeptically. "You would talk to me if you started feeling bad, wouldn't you?"

"Of course," I tried to sound convincing.

"I know I'm a little off the wall but, I mean, you have to keep your sanity in this business." He gave a second glance at me. "No offense."

"It's okay. I feel fine."

I crawled back into my room and then went downstairs to watch some TV. My room didn't feel like my room with Dalton lurking outside.

Chapter 26

For the rules to come from the antoherings that it come fromt to followthine things that syous see . . .

Things are going faster now. Broken-hearted lumps of clay that I mold into what they want to be. Broke a string or two on my guitar. Gotta get it fixed. Maybe strumming it too hard. I like its pearl inlay. I play guitar, you know. Play it faster. I've picked up the tempo of "The Angel of Saint Jude" to see how fast I can play it. When I play it real fast, it sort of sounds like it's Mexican. I like it that way.

Somehow, I managed to graduate. Teachers felt sorry for me. I know that was it. Mr. Cooke usually gives out ten pages of homework a day, but he only gives me ten pages a week. Under the table so no one knows it. I ran across the stage. Principal tossed me the diploma like it was a relay race. People laughed. I beamed. Catch me if you can.

Saw a really nice outfit in the window of the store to buy, but I didn't have any money. Went in to see if they'd let me apply for a credit card but they didn't. Big Mama looking at me funny.

I went to the campus in Asheville today. It was a part of one of those tours. I planned to start school in the fall. Mom had to work, but Big Mama drove me there and offered to walk around with me, but I decided the last thing I needed was her following me like a prison matron after me. Besides, I wanted to check out the guys.

The university was quaint, filled with old brick buildings that reeked of home, and someone told me James Madison had stayed in one of the dormitories. But I thought that unlikely, the university was founded fifty years after Madison was dead. Still, it made a nice story.

The music department was what I wanted to see, and as I walked down the narrow hallways, I peered through the windowed slate of glass in the door to see students practicing, in rooms I hoped would one day have room to hold my songs.

I was walking across campus when I saw Blaine standing near a bunch of guys, the big burly type that looked like football players. Blaine's slender frame was out of place. But it didn't matter to me. I would be in his rich arms . . . honey, milk and dew. I forgot myself and ran to him.

"Blaine."

He looked at me, but his glance grazed off me, returning to his friends. I came closer. I called louder.

"Blaine, it's me!"

His eyes were empty, as if he didn't recognize me.

"Oh, come on. You haven't forgotten me already? You've forgotten all the nights on the fire escape? It's me, Taylor!" I laughed and stopped in its tracks any conversation he was having with the other guys.

"Who?" his eyes steamed.

"Taylor," my voice cracked. "We stayed at—"

Before I could finish the sentence, he grabbed me by the arm and whisked me away from the group. His fingers pinched the inside of my arm a little too tightly and I squealed.

"Don't you dare say a word," he hissed through clenched teeth. "Don't you dare say 'Saint Jude' on this campus."

"Okay, okay, calm down."

"What are you doing here?"

"Looking at colleges, what do you think?"

"You can't come here."

"Why not? They have a decent music department."

"I mean, you can't come here because you're from there."

"What?"

"I don't want you here because you're from that place."

"Saint Jude?"

"Dammit, I told you not to even say it."

"What's going on?"

"Look, if anybody asked, I didn't see you, understand? I don't even know you."

"Did you forget to take your medication?"

"Don't say that. No one here knows about it, and that's the way it's going to stay."

"What are you talking about?"

"My illness. No one knows."

"That's nice, but it's really not a big deal . . ."

"That's what you think."

"Blaine, this is not you. What happened to that, 'I'm me and screw all the rest of them' philosophy that you were so famous for?"

"It died."

"What part of you died?"

"The insane part."

"What else died?" I was afraid to say it. "Did the part that loved me also die?"

"It's all so different when you're in college. You wouldn't understand. It's not that simple anymore."

"What do you mean?"

"No boundaries."

"New friends . . ."

"Those guys were in the fraternity I want to join. If word gets out that I'm schizo, they'll blackball me."

"But word will get out, Blaine. Word always gets out."

"Shut up, Taylor. For God's sake, just shut up!"

"What happened to you?"

"The world happened to me, Taylor. The world happened to me, that's what."

"I don't understand."

He rubbed his thoughtful eyes and shook his head. "You exhaust me, Taylor. Good God, how you exhaust me . . ." His voice seemed to tune in and out—almost as if it didn't belong to him anymore. "You want to know about the world? Let me tell you.

"I was at this party. One of the brothers invited me because I seemed like an okay guy and he heard I was pretty good with a basketball. It was the typical college scene: beer, and babes, and there's this homeless man out in the back by the dumpster. He looks homeless anyway. He's dressed in rags and old newspapers and just shuffles around like an old shoe. Anyway, he came up to the porch of the house, mumbling to himself. I looked him straight in the face and he started to drool. I knew that look . . .

"It was a look I had on many occasions. When you're so doped up on your illness that you don't have any room for any reality. He was crazy. I knew it because I was crazy, too. Then this soccer player named Mark, says, 'Watch this . . .' and he grabs the guy over his shoulders and goes up to the third floor. There he pushes him out the window, holding him only by his ankles. He laughed as the man struggled and clawed at the bricks in fright. He held him out there forever.

"The worst part of all is I had to laugh with them. I knew if they found out about me, it would be me hanging out the window. So I just laughed. Like it was all a part of their game, and madness suddenly had a new definition. Taylor, we aren't the ones who are insane; they are. But we've got to keep a lid on it or they'll destroy us."

"What happened to the homeless man?"

"They brought him back inside the house."

"See, Blaine? People can learn, and you can teach them. They've probably just never met someone with a mental disorder and don't know how to react. Think of the difference you could make in their thinking, their lives. You can't just blink it out, Blaine. You can't pretend that your illness doesn't exist because it does. It's there and nothing you can do is ever going to change that."

He turned to me sharply. He started to speak but anger flustered him so that he only started to sputter.

"Taylor, do you think . . ." He caught his breath. "Do you think the world gives a damn that you're mentally ill?"

"But you're living a lie."

"What? Just because I'm not going to be like Reno and blurt it like a trumpet to the entire free world? You're going to be like Reno, you're going to wear a big sign around your neck that says 'Help me, I'm a victim.'"

"Reno doesn't do that."

"Reno does exactly that."

"Reno knows who she is. She doesn't live a lie."

"Do you think the world is like Saint Jude? Do you think you're going to go out there and you're going to have some warm fuzzy therapist to hold your hand through life's wake? I'm here to tell you it's not that way. That's a stony dream, is what that is."

My hands had become very cold, and a wind was picking up. I reached out to touch him on the shoulder, just once more, so I could remember what my angel felt like.

Blaine let my fingers get just within reach, and then backed away, returning to his friends and his world, leaving me on the other side of the glass.

Chapter 27

If nothing everycomes fronmeif I can seewhat fasterofe the fasthinefaster . . .

I said nothing to Dalton as I entered the room, just like I said nothing to Big Mama on the way home. I bit at my nails until they bled. I kept tapping my foot against the glove compartment. Tap, tap, bleed, tap. Overdrive. Sail. Bite me.

"Taylor, how did . . ." I know Dalton started to ask "how did it go?" but the look on my face told him not to. "Wanna talk?" he raised his eyebrows behind the sports section of the Raleigh *News and Observer*. Dalton always read the *Observer*, even though in our town you could only get it a day late.

Upstairs, guitar. Had to play it out. Get the tune out of my head. It was all building around me. The waves had come back, and now they were darker and larger than ever. It haunted me like things you've swept under the carpet. Damn, broken strings. I broke Mom's favorite vase when I was five. . . got a whupping. Bam, bam, thank you ma'am. Damn him. Damn Blaine. Nothing new. Burning. He wouldn't hold me out the window, would he? He wouldn't drop me. Chords, loud. Strings, broken, Oh, damn. Damn.

I shut my door. Barricade. Isolate. Broken strings. It's all broken. Just like when I came to Saint Jude the first day. Everything's broken, and now I'm broken with them. Have to stay away. Barricade the door. Use the chair under the doorknob, use whatever. Smokeout. Lord, it's hot in here.

146

I was hot, burning. I felt my flesh against my cheek. It was a hurt. It was a promise. Would he really have married me? It was probably just another stony dream, too. No one would love me. Not someone as tattered and worn and used goods as me. I backed into the corner. I reached for my guitar—but it was so far away, and my hand was so small. My hand was so small. My hand was shrinking, if it was my hand. Guitar further away. A million miles away. Broken strings.

I tore at my blouse. It was hot and it stuck to my breasts. It was like heat, the sun searing on my chest. I ripped it off. Tore at it, threw it into the corner over my guitar. Had to break something, but what?

I stared at the shined steel plate that was a mirror. It was why my blush was either too heavy or too light and my lipstick never on straight. I never even attempted eyeliner.

My knuckles struck the smooth surface. I have to break my image. I was a mistake. Couldn't keep my parent's marriage together. Couldn't keep my songs together. Now I couldn't keep "The Angel of Saint Jude" together . . . I had broken God's angel. I could serve God best if I were dead. Knuckles. Pain. Hate the mirror. Kill the image. It had to break somehow. My face—it was so horrible. Dark circles under puffy eyes, breasts that were nonexistent, hair that was mousy and dull. I ripped at the hair, surprised to hear myself let out a yelp in pain.

"Taylor? Are you okay in there?" It was Big Mama. "Open the door."

She tried the door but realized it was jammed. Screw her. What did it matter now? Blaine was right. Everything about me was a mistake. I was illegitimate. In the end I wasn't even enough to hold my parent's marriage together. It was a disaster, I should have died and not my sister. She was the one they loved better.

"Taylor?" Big Mama's voice is a thousand miles away.

I see my feet as they stretch down into hell. The world is faster, so fast I can't keep pace. Big Mama trots downstairs.

It's almost as if I can hear Satan laughing at me. Not so loud at first, but just a faint chuckle as it splits my eyes into tears. I pounded my head against the wall. I kicked a hole in the wall. Cracks around the dry wall.

God, my face. My pimply, bloated, swollen, scowling face. No one could love me. No one would see me.

Why did I have to be different? Why can't my mind be still? I can no longer sleep! I stretch my soul forever, but it is not enough. God, why did you have to make me? I scratched my face savagely.

"Taylor!" It was Dalton. "I want you to open this door." He had pushed at it and now it was slightly cracked and he could see that I was tearing at my face. My eyes. I wanted to scratch them out so I wouldn't have to look at myself. But that would hurt. Pain was scary.

Loud cracks. Dalton breaks the door.

"Taylor . . ."

"Leave me alone!"

"I want you to stop clawing at your face."

"Go to hell!"

"Call the doctor," he said over his shoulder to Big Mama.

"I hate you!" Break down the wall. Battle of Jericho. And the walls come a-tumbling down. I wiped my cheek with the back of my hand. Blood. Knuckles were bleeding.

He walked slowly toward me, sneaky like, as if I couldn't see it. I throw my guitar at him. He dodges, but it clips his shoulder.

"Taylor, let's go for a walk."

"You don't care! It's burning! I'm not normal. Dear God, why am I a freak? I'm a damn freak! Freak, freak!"

He comes to me. I took a swipe at him. He caught my fist in mid-air. His grip was surprisingly strong. I kick his knee, he falls back. He's ruining everything. Bite, tear, claw, get away. Save the world. Get away from it. He was on me like a cat. He pulls my arms behind me and pins me to the ground, using his weight on top of me. I can't move. Jerk my head. Sweating, cursing. *Doesn't anybody else notice how hot it is in here?*

He keeps saying stuff to me, stuff that doesn't make sense. It's gibberish, running through me like glasses of water. I can't move. He yells for Big Mama. Tells her to do something—what I'm not sure—the world is spinning . . .

Chapter 28

We offer a comprehensive hospital referral guide so you can choose the best option . . .

I was sent to a private hospital about two hours away. It was slightly more expensive, but Dalton convinced Mom that they had the best adolescent care. The walls were a pale beige with Monet posters taped to them—an attempt to soothe the savage longings that had made their way into our soul. The men were on the other side of the ward, and it was rumored among the nurses that the genders weren't even separated until a romance gone awry led to a double suicide and a possible lawsuit.

This time a nurse checks my mouth to be sure that I swallow my pills, and they take my blood every day to ensure that the lithium is building itself back up in my bloodstream.

There's this one worker on the floor; an intern, and he's only about twenty-one. I resent the fact that he's only slightly older than me and yet he has authority over me. What's the difference in our ages? A few beers, that's all.

At first, they wouldn't even let me go to the bathroom by myself. I can't help it. I have a shy bladder. I can't pee with a nurse standing in the door. Sometimes she stares aimlessly at the walls, sometimes she brings a copy of the Asheville evening paper. They put me in a paper gown and had me isolated in suicide watch. They first took the restraints off as soon as it was decided that I wasn't going to freak.

And then there are the drugs.

So doped up at times that I have to use the handrail to walk down the hallway, like some elderly forgotten woman at a bad nursing home. I was taking Navane, which they told me was an anti-psychotic. They said one of the side effects was that it may cause me to start lactating. I haven't, but my breasts are swollen and larger and it hurts to put on a bra.

We ate in this place that was like a small snack area. It had a TV with a VCR, and in the evening we had to watch documentaries about how to live with your mental illness—I think it was a series that was done by the Surgeon General.

In addition to the locked doors that separated us from the men's ward, there was also a huge door that separated us from the truly psychotic patients. Although the hospital would deny it, these people were basically institutionalized, and were not going to get any better. The wall of their ward joined the wall for our snack room/cafeteria, and sometimes we could hear them screaming and pounding against the walls. It served as something the nurses could threaten us with.

"Don't act out or I'll put you in the other ward, and you don't want to go there," one of them had said to me when I griped about having to spend all day in seminars or making trivets. One girl on the hall told me that the worst thing about being on the other ward was the loneliness. Everyone over there is so out of touch with reality, you can't carry on a conversation with any of them, so you end up sitting there, staring at the walls, and all too soon you learn that you're in serious danger of contagion.

Dalton was primarily responsible for me getting out of there as soon as I did. He assured them of a strictly supervised environment and daily monitoring of lithium levels. He even said he'd do it himself if it needed to be done. That was when I found out that he was also a phlebotomist. (But he let his certification expire. I'm sure he didn't bother to tell them that.)

Chapter   29

We are always available to talk with you . . .

I avoided Dalton when I got back from the hospital. I was afraid his penetrating eyes would make me feel shame for kicking him and biting him. When he wore a short-sleeved shirt, I could still see the marks I gave him on his lower arm. We didn't talk until he called to me from my fire escape out the window.

He had that ever-present cigarette and cup of coffee; it was comforting to know some things never change.

"You feel better?" It was a question, but he phrased it as a statement.

"Much."

"That was a stupid thing you did. Could've gotten yourself killed."

"I know."

"Of course, thank God we were ready for it. I saw it coming."

"You did?"

"The fast talking, the lack of sleep—it was just a matter of time before something set you off to help you crash."

"If you knew I was going down that road, why didn't you stop me?"

"For what? I check under your tongue a couple of times to see if you've swallowed your pills, and then when you leave Saint Jude you do exactly what you want. No, it was better for you to learn your lesson when you were in a safe environment with people to get you to the hospital."

"I'm sorry . . . I mean, I know I kicked you."

"You bit me, too."

"I know, it's just that . . ."

"Don't worry about it. When I was in college, I worked as an orderly in an institution."

"I just felt so high."

"It's kind of like being a junkie, Taylor. You get addicted to those highs. But let me tell you, what goes up must come down." He lit up another cigarette. "You saw Blaine, didn't you?"

"He's in complete denial. Didn't even want to admit that he knew me. I mean, at one point we were so in love and now it's like I don't even exist."

"Sometimes people have to block out the dark parts in their lives. It's the only way they can deal with it."

"But it's not right."

"It's not a matter of it being right or wrong. It's a matter of how people deal with things. Taylor, you have to learn to let go."

"It's not easy."

"My girlfriend's back at Duke. Did I tell you that?"

"Yeah."

"She's not getting any better. They're even talking about some kind of brain surgery. I don't like it. Sounds too much like a lobotomy."

"They still do those?"

"Yeah, but they call them something else, now."

He put his arm around me and pulled me to his shoulder.

"I would've missed you, kid. Now it's just you and me and Big Mama."

"Why haven't they sent any more kids to Saint Jude? We haven't gotten a new admit since Princess left."

"Let me tell you something about the people that run Saint Jude. They are good, honest, God-fearing Christian people with

hearts of gold. However, they do not know what the hell they
are doing."

"What do you mean?"

"Psychologists these guys are not. They wanted to create
a safe haven for upper middle-class teens that had emotional
problems. Make it like a clubhouse with Mickey Mouse and
Kool Aid. It doesn't work that way. There are state regulations,
liability insurance, salaries, certifications—none of which these
people understand."

"You mean Saint Jude's isn't certified or whatever?"

"No, it is, it's just that they didn't exactly go through the
correct channels to get them. It's all in who you know. White
upper-class businessmen get whatever they want in this state."

He took a sip of coffee—long and deep like he was samp-
ling a first-class wine.

"No, Taylor, as soon as you get the okay to go, Saint Jude
will undergo a temporary shut down to give us time to get our
ducks in a row."

"Well, you'll be able to get them straightened out."

"Help? No way. I'm not going to stick around while a bunch
of yuppies debate their cause of the month. I'm going to see
my girlfriend. If she's okay, I might take her out on the town.
There's this great little Greek place . . " He hung his head,
his upper teeth curling their way around his lower lip. "I don't
love her, you know."

He said it plain and matter-of-factly, as if he were stating
his name.

"You don't?"

"No, Taylor. I'm in love with her disease. She was different. She was in trouble. I could help her. I suggested she go
to a shrink and then that opened up this big can of worms."

"If you don't love her, why are you engaged?"

"I know, I know, I should take the ring back, but I can't.
I would feel like I was abandoning her. Then one day I realized that if she ever did get well, we'd have nothing to talk

about. The whole relationship would just dissolve."

I needed to say something, but I didn't know what.

"It's such a shame, too," he said. "She's a good woman. She deserves far better than me."

"Do you think I'll be able to leave soon?" It was an easy way to change the subject.

"Taylor, you can only leave for as long as you take your medicine. Tell you what, late registration classes start up for Middlesex University in a couple of weeks. Inez teaches there. She could help you get into some good music classes."

But the money . . ."

"Didn't your dad leave you a bunch?"

"I don't want his handouts."

"Taylor, there are no handouts. You take what you can get. Saint Jude . . ." Here he gave a strange chuckle. "Do you even know who Saint Jude is?"

"No."

"He's the patron saint of lost causes. When you're praying and praying and you don't seem to be getting anywhere, then you pray for Saint Jude to intercede. Saint Jude, Christ. We're all lost causes, see, and half the time we're just hanging in for the ride."

He pulled away from me and started back inside.

"Tell you what, Taylor. I know that little medication fiasco wasn't all your doing. Blaine had a part in it, too. You show me that you can be responsible, and I'll write you a one-way ticket out of here."

"To go back home? I don't think so."

"No. To go to school."

"Where would I live?"

"I hear Middlesex just renovated the dorms."

Chapter 30

We fully believe that each of you will be able to live a fulfilling, independent life . . .

Middlesex was a private, Christian college where the rumor was they still had the ten-inch rule—men were not allowed to be within ten inches of a woman at any time, and if a man was visiting in your dorm room, the door had to be open at least ten inches. Rumor had it that some old schoolmarm went around with a ruler enforcing it.

But like every campus it had its own subculture. This was in a place called the Round Table. (The mascot was the Royal Knight.) It was a small loft just off campus where rumor had it that they watered down the beer.

Ironically, Inez hooked me onto the Round Table—not because she had a knack for partying or she wanted to introduce me to the wrong crowd, but they were always looking for new entertainment. Background music mostly. Just play softly in the background while life went on around you. It was a role I was well adept at playing. I used some of the money from Dad to get my guitar fixed, and my fingers returned to their old confidence on the strings, despite the fact that my knuckles still carried scars.

Inez had gotten me set up with some of the best professors, and though Dalton didn't really come out and say it, he implied to me that she had a heated affair going on with the college dean, which allowed her to get anything she wanted.

She even arranged for me to take a music class, although it was generally reserved for sophomores.

Although there was a strict rule regarding faculty-student faternization, Inez took it upon herself to introduce me to the manager of the Round Table.

"She has the best music potential since that Williams boy who came through in '73," she told him with a grin.

Someone later explained to me that Dan Williams went to Middlesex as a music major, played at the Round Table, and became a highly successful folk artist. Autographed pictures of him were all over the Round Table, and once a year he came back to perform for a major fundraiser for the university.

"I don't know. Williams was one of a kind," the manager had greasy hair and a graying goatee, which made him look like one of the strongmen you see at the circus.

"Give her a shot. First night, she plays for free. Thereafter, you pay her what you pay your regulars." I couldn't believe Inez was this bold.

"If I hire her."

"You'll hire her."

Yeah, that's great, Inez. No pressure there.

I loved my guitar but hadn't quite gotten to the point where I was comfortable playing in front of people—that old adage about imaging them all in their underwear never worked for me—and I didn't really want to go, but Inez said she would consider it a favor, and she had done so much to help me get set up, I felt that if I didn't I would offend her.

The place smelled of stale beer and cigarettes. Not exactly the place you'd expect to find near a Christian campus—but then they always say it's the son of a preacher man who's the wildest. As Inez said, Middlesex was usually where some of the wilder kids were sent, hoping that a more holy environment and chapel every Wednesday would straighten them out.

The stage was small, and if I closed my eyes, I felt dizzy and was sure that I would fall off into somebody's lap. There's a couple sitting two tables down from the stage, and I can tell they're arguing although I can't what they're saying. Their eyebrows are crossed at sharp angles, their hand movements are blunt and direct. They don't want to touch each other, for fear that they would break.

When I went up to introduce myself, the microphone gave some feedback, and I could already tell there was going to be a good dose of static on the speaker.

I was going to open with some classics, maybe some Dylan, but a voice inside told me to try something original. I hadn't played "The Angel of Saint Jude" since my breakdown; I felt that when Blaine had left me, the song went with him. I briefly debated whether or not I wanted to sing it, because I really didn't want to advertise the fact that I had a connection with Brick House. But they couldn't think I was any stranger than the waitress that was just emerging from the bathroom with a nose ring and a streak of fire engine red down the part of her hair.

The strings were cold and foreign. I rubbed my palm over them to get them reacquainted to me. They weren't used to the crowds. I would have to calm them down like they were a nervous horse.

I cleared my throat. It was dry and scratchy. Some people were starting to look at me, wondering if I really knew what I was doing. The couple in the corner continued to argue . . .

"Reading books late at night when he came through
      my window,
Hovered over my shoulder from dusk till dawn.
Kissed me on the forehead as he was leaving,
All that's left is feathers on the lawn.

I never knew who he was or why he came,
or why my tattered, broken life

will never be the same.
I think the world would be much better
if everybody knew
my guardian—the Angel of Saint Jude."

It was then that I noticed it.
The silence.
The conversation pockets had ceased. The requests from the bar were quieter and more discreet. Above the lights, I could make out eyes turning toward me. The couple in the corner had stopped fighting and turned to listen.

They listened. After years of shrinks and psychotherapy, someone finally listened.

Chapter 31

Mental illness is very common, although few are willing to talk about it . . .

It was halfway through the semester before Inez got me a spot in one of the dorms. It took so long because I wanted a single room. Dad had left the extra money, and the last thing I needed were hassles from a roommate and Inez agreed. I spent half the semester at Saint Jude with Dalton bussing me in. (Big Mama quit when she realized there wouldn't be any new admits. She told Dalton she had better things to do than wait on his sorry ass hand and foot.)

Dalton helped me pack up my things into boxes. He had very little else to do with no one at Brick House, but he said he'd stay there for as long as they'd pay his rent. Then he'd return to Duke to stay with his fiancée. But somehow, I didn't think he'd ever leave Asheville.

Mom offered to help me pack, but I told her that we had a handle on it. I'm needing her less and less now, just as she needs me less and less. I like to fantasize that maybe she'll hear one of my songs on the radio one day and then realize what a jewel she left behind. I don't dare tell that to anyone because they'd probably think I was becoming manic and increase my medication.

"You know, Taylor, when it comes down to it, life is just a matter of hanging on," Dalton said.

"Did you enjoy college?"

"What I remember of it."

"Do you think I'll become a guitarist?"

"I think you already are one."

"No, I mean a real one. One where I can make a living at it."

"It all depends upon what you mean by making a living. For some making a living is three cars, a pool and a membership to the country club. For others, it's a small apartment with orange crates."

One room. My room at Saint Jude. Could it really have held all that emotion? Remembering Reno, I moved the bed.

"Taylor, what are you doing?"

"Reno told me something was here. Before I leave, I want to see for myself."

Sure enough, underneath the bed were dark stains in the hardwood floor. Stains where Joan killed herself in that same room years ago. Stains that left Reno behind. I was afraid of seeing them before now—afraid that my blood would mingle with it. But now, it was okay. But was it okay with Reno? Did she ever get over it?

"Dalton, how's Reno doing?"

"I don't really hear much from her. She's seeing a private doctor last I heard. Her husband felt the doctors at the clinic were all idiots."

"Do you have her address and phone number?"

"In my files."

"Can I have it?"

Chapter 32

We ask that you utilize candor when you meet someone from Saint Jude outside the facility . . .

No one ever answered the phone at Reno's. I never got an answering machine, which surprised me; I thought I heard her mother say she had given her one for Christmas.

Once I thought I saw her at the Round Table, but it was someone from my anthropology class.

That Saturday I got a friend to take me down to Reno's housing development in the ritzy part of Asheville. It was outside of Biltmore Forest and was called Brickencourt Square. It was a yuppie heaven. I saw a woman jogging down the street in an outfit that probably cost more than my first semester tuition. New houses were springing up like anxious children. They were painted with boldly-colored shutters and house numbers done in porcelain block numbers from Mexico.

Her house number was easy to remember—1492. The year that Columbus discovered the New World.

"Who is it?" Reno's muffled reply came over the intercom.

"It's me, Taylor."

The door cracked at first, and cautious eyes peered from around the corner, as if she were afraid to believe. Then, without warning, the door burst open and arms encircled my neck.

"It's you!" she squealed. "It's really you!" Her hands ran over my face and my hair. "Come in—of course, I haven't vacuumed—the maid only comes on Wednesdays—but come in.

Man, how I've missed you!"

The apartment was cluttered with old magazines and stray flakes of kitty litter that decorated the kitchen floor.

"Sit down." She cleared a spot on the couch, jerking the cat out of the way. "So where are you now?"

"Middlesex University."

"Wow. That's expensive. The private college. I hear there are some hot guys there." She was wearing a black tank top—the apartment was like a sauna. "I'll get you a Coke." She turned and sauntered toward the refrigerator.

It was then that I noticed it.

Dark and blue on her right shoulder, a bruise that ran down the side of her arm.

"You've gotten banged up a bit," I said. "What happened?"

"So how many classes are you taking?"

"I'm going full time, but I'm taking really easy courses. Inez said it was best not to push it."

"Hmm," she stopped halfway between the couch and the fridge and stared into space. "Inez was the best. She made me feel like a real person. I'd give anything to see her again."

"Why don't you come down to the college with me? We could all do lunch."

"It's not that simple anymore. When you're married, things change."

"What do you mean?"

"It's just not simple anymore, that's all. You can't always do the things you want."

"Where's Tim?"

'He's at work—working part time at a construction site. His dad likes for him to get his hands dirty instead of sitting in the office all day. He's the guy who directs the traffic."

Something about the bruise bothered me. I saw another one below her elbow.

"Seriously, how did you get so banged up? You playing pick-up basketball?"

She laughed, but it was a laugh unlike any kind I've ever heard before. It'd lost its magic, the lilt that made it Reno's. This was a laugh that could have belonged to anyone, not the clever, uplifting chuckle I had always expected with Reno.

"I slipped," she said. "I fell down the steps."

"Where?"

She gave that unfamiliar laugh again and took a sip of the Coke that she had originally gotten for me.

"Isn't that what you always say? You fell down the steps. Doesn't matter if you live on the first floor. It doesn't even matter if you're in a wheelchair. We always use the steps, as if they're going to allow us to climb our way out of here."

"What are you talking about?"

"Tim likes to play rough. It started after we'd been married a couple of weeks. No biggie. Just pulling my hair if he'd had a particularly bad day at work. Then he'd slap me—not hard. Then he knocked me up against the wall . . "

"Good Lord, Reno, what are you doing here?"

'It's like Jeckyll and Hyde, man." She put her arm around me. "I knew you were always too smart to fall for that stairs thing. It sounds hokey, but at least it keeps my mom from asking questions."

"So when are you moving out?"

"What?"

"When are you moving? You could stay with me in my dorm. I've got a single."

"I'm not leaving him."

"What?"

."It's not that bad, really. I mean, it's not ideal, but every marriage has its problems. At least he's clean. He doesn't sleep around or do drugs," she chuckled.

"This is not funny."

"Actually, Taylor," she took a deep drink of my Coke. "it is funny. Funny as hell. To think that I would end up with such a situation like this."

"Why can't you leave him?"

"Where would I go? Back to Mommy—who put me away in Saint Jude's to keep me from being a delinquent? No, she'd just say that I got what I deserved."

"Is that what you believe?"

"I don't know. I think life deals you some tough cards, and you've got to play them."

Was this the same Reno that orchestrated the attack on the student nurses and organized Castaway meetings?

"Reno, what happened to you?"

"I was so afraid of not belonging," she said. "I thought I could keep up this act. For awhile I enjoyed being crazy. It was freedom from responsibility. Then I moved out and responsibility found me."

"Is that what Tim was for?"

"Who knows?"

"There's this place where you could get a job. It's called the Round Table—"

"Doing what? Waiting tables? No thanks. Tim may be a jerk but he's got me set up. I have a private doctor now. I don't see the ones at the clinic."

"Have you been taking your medicine?"

"My medicine," Reno leaned very close to my face. "It's the only thing that keeps me from blowing my brains out."

"You can make a move—"

"With what? I've got no education."

"I thought you had your GED."

"An elaborate orchestration to get me the hell out of there. I knew Dalton was my chance. He wanted to get rid of us as bad as we wanted to get rid of him."

"Dalton's okay," I felt almost compelled to defend him.

"Yeah, I guess, but Tim's okay, too, you've got to realize that. Maybe my life isn't perfect, but I've got a maid on Wednesday, expensive scotch in the cabinet . . ."

"I never knew Tim was so high profile. . ."

"He is."

". . . or so low class."

"Taylor, I only told you this because I don't want you to judge me. It's my life. "I'll handle it."

"But you could be so much more."

"What? Taylor, I can't let Mom support me all my life. Brick House nearly wiped her out. If I got a job, it wouldn't be something where I could afford my present shrink."

"You could go to the clinic."

"The clinic," she said, shaking her head. "The clinic is how I ended up at Saint Jude."

The phone rang. As she spoke into the receiver, her face fell. Perhaps sensing that I might have noticed, she turned with her back to me.

We had all walked a fine line—Isaac, Princess, Reno, Blaine and I. Isaac and Princess had lost their hand, and Blaine and Reno had made it to the real world. Somehow, I wondered if Reno and Blaine were any better off for making it to reality. The whole world was crazy, and crazy people trying to make it in a crazy world was more than I wanted to think about.

Was it better to live or to be safe? Was it better to risk? It's like being posed at the edge of a cliff. Most people would rather stand still, because if you took a chance at flying, you also took a chance at falling.

Now the table turned to me. It was all a big crap shoot, and where you ended up, only God knew.

I didn't realize that she had put down the phone.

"Taylor, I hate, hate to do this, but Tim's coming home on his lunch break. He wants to take me to look at this new hot tub he wants to put in," she paused again and gave a breathless laugh that sounded like a whimper. "A damn Jacuzzi."

"I could tag along."

"No, no. Tim likes to be the center of attention. If not, he gets a little, well . . ."

"I have every right to report him."

"For what? You can't prove anything. Neither can I. Don't you read about these women? The women who report things and end up dead in the street the next day?"

"That's not going to be you."

"Damn straight it's not. It's not because I'm playing my cards right."

"Reno—"

"It's not bad. When I was growing up, I got worse bruises from falling off the monkey bars."

"But don't you see? It will get worse."

"Dammit, Taylor, think about what you're saying. I go to court. I get on the stand. What's the first thing that comes up? Oh, I've been at Saint Jude. Oh, I'm crazy. Now who are they going to believe: a guy whose father is a respected business-man in Asheville or a girl who needs a Prozac the size of a watermelon?"

"But it's not right."

"But who's on my side, Taylor? Not the law. They get tired of the paperwork. Not my friends. They think I'm weak be-cause I don't leave. Not the lawyers. They're just in it for a buck. Not the shrinks or doctors. They practically get a com-mission. So who's on my side Taylor? Who's on my side?"

"I am."

"Sorry, but you're not enough."

Chapter 33

Finally, we ask that you remember the words of William Yeats: "Nothing can be made whole, that was not torn or rent."

I thought about her words between shuffles of papers, trying to figure out why I got a 'C' on the exam if this was supposed to be an easy class. I saw her face in every couple that visited the Round Table.

After a set, the manager gave me one of his fried cheese specials and a beer—even though I was underage. I stared awkwardly at it for awhile. The only time I had tasted beer was when my Dad let me take a sip of his when I was five and he was watching the ACC basketball tournament—I went to the bathroom and promptly threw up.

"It's from that man over there," the manager gestured to the table in back.

I didn't recognize Dalton at first. It was as if his whole face had changed. Rings of smoke hung around his face like tarnished halos, his bright eyes sagged with grayness around the edges and somewhere I felt his spirit must have left him.

"What are you doing here?" I asked.

"I came to tell you to come out tomorrow and get the rest of your stuff."

"Stuff?"

"Yeah, a few dresses, some toiletries, that sort of stuff. I would've packed it for you but I didn't want to go snooping through your things."

"I wouldn't mind."

He smiled. "Respect for your privacy keeps me from going through your stuff."

"Why the big rush? I mean, I had wanted some things there just in case, God forbid, I would have to go back."

"Forget it, kid. It ain't gonna happen."

"I appreciate your confidence in me."

"No, I mean it's not going to happen. Saint Jude is closing."

It was like losing your pocketbook. You don't really miss the money or credit cards as much as you miss the pictures you kept in your wallet. I had no pictures of Brick House. During my entire stay, no one had ever taken a picture. Now that it was gone, I had nothing to remember it by.

"I'm having lunch with Inez. I can stop by and pick it up then. She wants me to play my songs for her."

"Inez believes in you. You better stick with her. Better treat her like the Queen of Sheba."

I nodded. "You believe in me, too."

"Yeah, well . . ."

"Reno has no one to believe in her!" It blurted out, dark and crass, like my worn voice. "He's beating her, Dalton, and she won't leave!"

"I couldn't put my finger on it, but I had a bad feeling about that guy."

"Then why did you let her leave?"

"Because every so often, you have to let go. You spend all your time nurturing patients, you work with them, and then one day, they come in and say, 'I don't need you anymore.' You know it's not true. You know they're going to step out of the office and they're going to walk face first into the real world and it's going to hit them like a ton of bricks. But you can't do anything, Taylor. You've got to let them go. Because if you don't, you're just as bad as the people who put them there in the first place."

The manager made a motion with his arm, and my break

was over. It was time for another set. I told Dalton I'd see him to-morrow. He gave a light nod and puffed away at his cigarette.

"How long have you been smoking?"

"Since I was fifteen."

"That stuff's going to kill you."

"I'm not afraid of dying. Living is scarier."

I resisted the urge to move the bed and take another look at the bloodstains on the floor in Joan's old room. It reminded me too much of Reno. I looked out at the junkyard. The pale Pinto was gone. I had hoped that instead of being sold for parts, that someone had found use for it. Inez was waiting for me in the car.

"Need any help?" Dalton asked as I stuffed what was left into my duffel bag.

"No, I got it."

"Got big plans for declaring a major?"

"Not yet. I love my guitar, but I know I'm going to have to play a lot of gigs before I get somewhere, and playing in bars just isn't my thing."

"Not your style?"

"Bars are sad places. People looking for something, and they aren't even sure where to get it."

"I've got a job in Durham," he said.

"At another group home?"

"No, no. Lord, no. It's at a clinic, counseling people who just got out of a mental hospital. Kind of a decontamination chamber before the real world."

"Kind of like Saint Jude."

"I guess."

"And your girlfriend?"

"And my girlfriend . . . we'll just take it a step at a time." Then he broke into a grin. "Enough of this. Come here, you."

He hugged me and kissed me lightly on the forehead.

I shuffled down the steps. The house no longer hummed to me. Soon it would be used for Bible studies and senior citizen breakfasts. They'd never know about the bloodstains under the bed, the conversations on the fire escape, or how if you hit the vending machine right, you could get candy for free.

But where was Reno's voice in all of this? She was there for me at Saint Jude and now I had to be there for her. I could be a lawyer. I could be the one asking her the questions on the stand. I could be on her side, and this time, I would be enough.

I gave a last glance at the living room, the TV on which Blaine wanted to play dirty movies, the chair where a vexed Princess filed her fingernails, the hallway where Isaac cried . . .

The front porch no longer creaked beneath my weight, as if I had suddenly grown lighter while at Saint Jude. The windows were still dirty, and the porch still needed a fresh coat of paint, but these were not chores to be done by the Brick House crew.

With a deep breath I threw my duffel bag on my shoulder. Then, without looking back, I left Saint Jude.